MAR

All The Thin
The Thing I

ANOTHER SMALL PRESS

No.1

Copyright © Martin Costello 2023
All rights reserved

ISBN 978-0-9957127-0-6

Published in Great Britain by Another Small Press, 2023

www.anothersmallpress.net
Cover design by Fine Fine Lines

The story the author had always been trying to write is not included in this collection but happily is now complete after 22 years of editing.

Martin Costello lives in the East Midlands.

Contents

Fools' Errand	7
Cumulative Song	18
As Day Follows Night	24
Deterge	28
Muttonhead	30
I Could've Killed You Back There	34
Colloquium	36
What Happened At The Ossington	68

Fools' Errand

A Bag of Sparks

In West Berkshire we made a list of the things we would need for an adventure in the Netherlands. Godwin Timms packed a bag full of smaller bags. Some of the smaller bags had even smaller bags inside of them, and some of the even smaller bags had tiny bags inside of them. So inside his main bag – which wasn't even a very big bag itself – were many, many small bags of different sizes. "Do you have enough small bags for this trip, Godwin?" I asked. He told me that he thought he probably did. He also packed five empty plastic cartons with resealable lids and two packets of sweets. I wondered if perhaps two packets would not be enough, but as it happened, we only used one. I still have the other, just in case, all this time later. "Are you taking anything else?" I asked him.

"I have a map of The Hague," he said, "although it is very small, and Dutch. And it is thirty years old, so some of the roads may have changed. What about you – do you have the book?"

I did have the book. In fact I had two books – one full of stories and one full of lists. "This one," I said, "is full of lists. On page forty-nine is a list of things we should be looking out for in the Netherlands. With this, and your tiny map, we should not lose ourselves."

"Unless we want to," said Godwin. He was right. We could do that if we wanted to. Once we had found Hermannus, which was our first priority.

"Well then," I said, "it looks like we have everything. We should go. You can drive, and I will look out for a woman under a hedge, which is on the list." Godwin asked me if it would count, seeing a woman under a hedge in England, when really, the list was for our trip in the Netherlands. I thought about it. "As long as it's a Dutch woman, I think so, yes."

A Moral Compass

Godwin Timms had never met Hermannus, so he didn't know precisely what he was looking for when I invited him to join me on the search for Hermannus one day last year in the middle of winter. But Godwin knew this: you don't have to know what you are looking for in order to find it. Sometimes, of course, when you do know what you are looking for, you never find it anyway. It seemed a perfectly reasonable idea to accompany me to the Netherlands in the search for Hermannus. It was A Very Important Trip, and the outcomes were uncertain. Not least because Hermannus might not be easy to find. He was the sort of fellow who might fall between the cracks in the pavement, or blow away in a winter wind, be lost in the fog or disappear into the shadows. All we had to go on was the last place I had seen him, a year before, and some very unsavoury rumours.

We planned to go straight to the seafront when we arrived in the Hook of Holland, as soon as we got off the ferry, to call on Hermannus in the coffee shop on the Pier where he had been working. But I began the search in advance, on the ferry from Harwich, when I met a man from The Philippines who was working as a waiter. He told me he lived in The Hague, so it was natural for me to ask if he had seen Hermannus recently, or knew of his whereabouts, or could vouch for his wellbeing. But Waiter Lionel had no information that was of any use, so Godwin bought a pitcher of beer from him, and we did not trouble him further.

In the early hours of the morning I took a stroll up on the deck, where I saw a man with a woman behind him. I checked my list, on page forty-nine of the book of lists, and as I suspected, such a scene was on the list. But when I asked a steward if we were nearly on the Dutch coast, he was quite sure that as yet we were in International Waters, and so it did not count.

Tulip Powder

It was raining in the Hook of Holland when we drove off the ferry, and it reminded me of the last time I was here, nearby, with a wind blowing off the water and sea spray in my eyes. Godwin was very quiet, perhaps because we didn't know what we were going to find when we caught up with Hermannus, or perhaps because of the pitcher of beer the night before. I thought it would be quite easy to find a man or woman walking, to get us started on the list, but in the grey dawn light, and the rain, no-one was about – the Hook of Holland was deserted. "I think we should stop at a petrol station and ask the first person we see to tell us what they know about Hermannus" said Godwin.

"That is a good idea, and here comes a petrol station now, but I think you should do the asking," I said to him, "because your Dutch is better than mine." Godwin explained that although he knew the correct words for chocolate sprinkles and pea soup, he mostly otherwise was probably no more fluent than I.

When he came back to the van he told me that the manager of the petrol station was there, but he did not know anything about Hermannus. He had advised Godwin to drive closer to The Hague, where people were more knowledgeable about such things. Godwin had bought two bottles of spring water to keep the manager happy, but considering the lack of information, we agreed it was something of a waste. We carried on toward Scheveningen, and though we saw nobody who might've been on our list, we did at least spot a flock of geese and some sheep, which brightened us both up, because it felt like we had really got started now.

Pig's Eggs

We got to the pier so early that the whole place was locked behind rusty iron gates, and Godwin shook them gently, perhaps hoping to shake off the lock, or to alert someone of our presence. But no-one was forthcoming. Finally at least, there were people beginning to appear on the windy seafront, and walking along the promenade we very soon spotted a man walking, a man with a woman behind him, and a man, woman and child in a buggy. We agreed we were in the wrong century to have much hope of spotting a post chaise, and that a Volkswagen would suffice. I saw a Polo almost straightaway. So far there was no sign of Hermannus, but at least we were getting through our list. I tried to stop a jogger to ask him if we could expect to meet our target, tall handsome Hermannus, on the pier when it opened, but he brushed past me, probably swearing in Dutch. Godwin reminded me that I should not take offence, for the Dutch were characteristically brusque, and besides which, it was impolite to stop a man at his exercise.

We went for breakfast.

We had window seats at the seafront café so that we could watch the rain drench the grey seas, and keep an eye out for a parson riding a grey horse, with blue furniture. And for Hermannus, of course. Speaking of which, I called over the waitress and asked her, "have you seen Hermannus lately?" She did not seem to know what I was talking about, although we had already established that she had a good grasp of English. I explained I was referring to the Hermannus who served coffee on the pier, but still, she did not know. We had eggs and hams and cheeses for breakfast, and waffles with honey – all you can eat for €10 – with orange juice, tea and coffee. It did not stop raining, and though we kept a close watch, taking turns at the buffet, we saw no sign of Hermannus.

Godwin and I had a short conversation about Escher, who was a famous resident of The Hague, and commented on aspects of our breakfast, which we found almost entirely agreeable.

10′ of Shoreline

It was time for the pier to open. "Shall we wait until the weather is more clement, do you think?" I asked Godwin, but it had been raining the last time we were here, a year ago, and it was raining now, and therefore it had probably rained all that time in between, so the chances of it not raining any time that day were slim, in Godwin's opinion. I had one last fried egg on a warm pancake and then we proceeded to the pier. As we passed the rusty iron gates which were now pulled open, I had a strong sense that we would not find Hermannus on the pier, and that our trip to The Netherlands would be a wasted trip.

We walked the length of the pier, and I could not be sure which of the glass-fronted units that ran along the centre of the structure had been a coffee shop. But whichever one it had been, it was no longer. I asked a vendor of confectionary and she directed us to an empty unit. Except it was not quite empty: the fixtures and fittings were gone, but an amphibious matt green military vehicle was parked inside the glass-fronted shop. I asked her, "have you seen Hermannus lately? Do you know where he is?" but she shook her head nervously, and explained that the woman who owned the shop had left at the end of last summer.

"You have summers in Holland?" asked Godwin, surprised, as if they only occurred in West Berkshire and the equatorial regions. I explained to the confectioner that we had no interest in the woman who had owned the shop, unless she could lead us to Hermannus, but she shrugged and went back to her sweet stall.

Godwin and I asked everyone on the pier that morning if they had seen Hermannus, or knew of his whereabouts, even the diver who was in the business of conserving the local crustaceans. He wanted us to buy a DVD of his adventures under the pier, and although we thought about it, we declined. After all, it was information we were looking for, not entertainment. It was Hermannus we were looking for, not crabs.

A Horse-Feather Pillow

I wrote a note for Hermannus, and pushed it through a gap in the locked sliding glass door of the old coffee shop, explaining precisely the nature of our visit and urging that tall charming man to get in touch with me at his convenience, although I doubted the note would ever find him. Godwin found an unspent match in the runner of the door, and carefully picking it up with a pair of tweezers, put it into one of his tiny bags, which he had to rummage for in his bigger bag. "It's a good job you brought all those tiny bags with you," I told him "there are bound to be more like that." I don't know why I said it, because Godwin did not need to be reassured. We took turns being photographed in the booth at the entrance to the pier, filmed a crack in the door of the former coffee shop, and finally decided it was time to go outside again.

Further up the promenade near the sand dunes and the grand old hotel, Godwin stepped in some dog faeces – accidentally – and while he was washing it off, standing there in the filthy weather with one bootless foot held up off the watery floor while he scrubbed the sole of his boot in a puddle and poked at it with a stick, I spotted a most unlikely thing. A parson on a grey horse with blue furniture. We stood in the rain and stared, Godwin hopping reverently with one boot in his hand and a dirty stick in the other, our mouths open and drips on our noses and in our eyebrows, like startled statues. The parson rode on by and proceeded to exercise the horse on the sands, while we wondered if, after all, we might see a woman under a bush, which would complete our list. It was early on our first morning, and anything seemed possible as we watched the horse canter along the beach for sport.

Later I would remember to explain to Godwin that I have a certain mystic power which I am quite unable to properly understand: that I have never, and somehow can never, tread in the unhealthy leavings of dogs. Even when I walk with my head held high and my eyes on the vista ahead, and even though the ground may be strewn with mess, my uncanny power will guide me cleanly on by. "What about fox mess?" asked Godwin. I told him I wasn't sure, but with the fox being canine, probably. "What about badger droppings?" Godwin asked me about many species, and some I could only speculate on, and overall, I was most uncertain. Only dogs and their nearest relatives, I felt. "Hyenas?" he asked.

A Portable Hole

In the afternoon the rain eased up somewhat, and having checked into our hotel and rested for an hour, we were revitalised and ready to start again on our search for Hermannus. We headed into the city centre of The Hague, where we soon came across a man whose job was to stand quite still with a large billboard pointing toward a kebab shop. So far we had asked about twenty people if they knew where we could find Hermannus, but information was not forthcoming, and being a busy city, the citizens of Den Haag were busy too. But the man with the sign looked like he could do with the conversation, and so we approached him cordially. His name was Kamran Dalstra of Groningen and he said he was having a nice day. Then Godwin offered to perform a magic trick to inject a little fun into his work place.

The trick is called Circle of Truth.

Kamran Dalstra of Groningen wrote a word on a small piece of paper, inside a circle drawn by Godwin. We asked him to make sure it was an English word, because truth or no, it was no good to us in Dutch, unless by unlikely chance it was the word for pea soup. We did not see what the word was. Kamran folded the paper up small and under Godwin's instruction, tore it into tiny pieces and threw them away. He was then told to answer many random questions and to say 'yes' as the answer to all of them. Even if it was not the right answer. Godwin gazed into his eyes and asked many questions, like "Is white a colour?" and "can camels canoe?" and "do you know where Hermannus is?" Godwin studied him carefully as he answered many questions, such as "have you seen a woman under a bush?" and "are hyenas related to dogs?"

Finally, Godwin correctly identified that the secret word Kamran Dalstra of Groningen had written down was 'north', and Kamran was both impressed by the trick and brightened so that he redoubled his efforts at standing still holding a big sign with renewed vigour. When we were out of his sight, Godwin opened up the tiny circle of paper on which Kamran had written 'north' and imagined he had thrown away. We were agreed it was a very significant word, since we were searching for someone who was lost, and that the circle of truth had worked out very well for everyone concerned. Godwin put the little piece of paper into a tiny bag, and sealed it.

Glass Nails

For the rest of the afternoon we undertook a search for clues and inspiration and encouragement concerning the hunt for handsome Hermannus, by scanning the ground carefully. It was a change of tactic, since we felt that the people of The Hague were not being straight with us concerning the whereabouts of our quarry. Godwin especially is a gifted finder of trinkets and significant ephemera, and it seemed the natural progression of the investigation to extend our search to the floor, where we might find things. Things that would point to Hermannus. By the wisdom of Kamran Dalstra we proceeded in a northerly direction. At every turn, when we discovered a new thing, Godwin would take out his tweezers and a tiny bag, and carefully place the item into his safekeeping. We made a mental note of each thing, to see if there was rhyme or reason to it, but we were not overly concerned to discover the truth of it there on the street, since we intended to take all the objects back to the hotel, where we could label them, and lay them out, and look at them contemplatively, in order to find the message in them.

Among the many things we discovered: a Wilhelmina Mint, some rivets, a shiny washer, a rusty badge pin, a glass bead, a broken bracelet, a padlock, unidentifiable samples of tin, copper, pewter, and stained steel pressed into the texture of the street by people stepping on them, a five-pointed star, some very small denomination coins, ticket stubs for tram and theatre, a key that did not fit the padlock, a shopping list, several circles and a rectangle, a love heart, a hinge and bracket, a costume ring, a shard of transparent coloured plastic, a button, a coiled spring, a miniature Buddha statuette, a fragment of red ribbon, a nail, and a number of small things with no easy explanation.

Universal Solvent

At the hotel we gave thought to our findings. We thought on it and stared for many minutes. Hours, even.

Plainly, Hermannus was not to be discovered. It was almost as if he was hiding from us, though he surely did not know we had come for him. For example, on the pier at Scheveningen the stall holders, confectioners, tobacconists, divers, and various others shrugged their shoulders dismissively and would speak only of the woman who owned the coffee shop now closed. Of Hermannus they declared almost no knowledge, and looked at us suspiciously. Another example, in the centre of The Hague: people claimed not to know what – or who – we were talking about. Even Kamran, who said he knew Hermannus because Godwin made him say it for the circle of truth, could not give us much detail, except the word 'north' which we suspected he just made up on the spot. The array of small items we picked up off the street yielded up new messages, none of them about the tall handsome man from the pier.

I told Godwin that I feared Hermannus would give us the slip, and he agreed the best thing we could do, in the circumstances, would be to head to Amsterdam, and the Nine Streets, where we might find some new adventure to take our minds off the present one. "We can save Hermannus for another day," he said, "after all, in our line of work, we are sure to come across him, eventually." I thought it was an optimistic assessment, but then, that is the difference between Godwin and I. The next day we proceeded to Amsterdam, where we found many unusual things in the flea market, and on the Nine Streets a Haphazard Bazaar so engaging that we forgot our troubles, for the time being.

A Curve Straightener

After two days it was time to come home. We had given up our search for Hermannus, and though we kept our eyes peeled for a woman under a bush, there was no sign of one. We brought back many items in tiny plastic bags, and some cartons of small things from Amsterdam. We had some new stories, and a plan (or two, if you count the map of Shang Hai I bought from the Haphazard Bazaar).

At the checkpoint at the Hook of Holland we had one last adventure, when a customs officer called Manuela disagreed with our assessment of the size of our van. "This is a van," she told Godwin, sternly, "and on my computer it says MPV. Can you explain this?" Godwin tried to explain it by suggesting Manuela was wrong. But she was not so much wrong as pig-headed, and was inclined not to let us on the ferry until we admitted it was a van, and not an MPV. One day, said Godwin to me, under his breath, this will be the woman under a bush.

Manuela forced Godwin to admit we were driving a van, and when this was done, we were permitted to board the ferry back to England. Only when we were back in West Berkshire did it occur to me that I still had both books, the one full of stories, and the one full of lists. I had intended to come home with only one. "Well then," said Godwin, "you will just have to post it."

"That," I replied, would make the whole thing a fool's errand. Better to keep it, and when we finally do run across Hermannus, we shall know what to do."

Cumulative Song

XII

"Where do you think you're going?!"

On the first day of his job as a supermarket delivery driver, this particular delivery driver was not about to be let off so lightly by the old man at the riverbank cottage. He had been warned this might be a difficult stop and sure enough, the old man wanted him to wait while he checked the contents of his grocery box. There wasn't much in it.

"One drum of coffee!" said the old man, begrudgingly satisfied. The driver was satisfied too - he didn't have to wait around for customers to check their groceries: they could always get refunds or redeliveries later, almost no questions asked, whenever drops turned out to be incorrect. His supervisor had told him not to tolerate any nonsense from Mr. Husk, a regular misery, who in any case would never be satisfied whatever you did for him. But this driver, a new man on the job, thought the odd kindness here and there or a showing of good will could never do any harm so waited patiently for the inspection to complete. For his part, the old man William Husk slammed his front door shut without further comment.

XI

On his second visit to the cottage on the riverbank, a late winter flurry had pushed back at the spring and the steep icy lane down to the river was treacherous. The delivery driver, delayed at every turn from the very start of his round, more or less slid down the slope to the cottage at the very back end of his delivery slot, and William Husk was waiting impatiently at his gate for his grocery box. He seemed a little under-dressed for this unexpected cold snap.

"Are you some kind of feckless idle layabout? Look at the time!"

His supervisor had warned him that Mr. Husk could be free with his insults and if he found they leaned into racial slurs - which he must report at once - he was not obliged to drop the food parcels and should immediately leave the scene. Though he had never heard the term 'feckless idle layabout' he was quite sure it wasn't worth depriving the old man his groceries. In fact he suspected it a rather antiquated dismissal of one's character and overlooked it with a smile. This feisty old fellow was funny, in his way.

He checked his groceries. The delivery driver was happy to wait for this short exercise before getting on his way, despite the time and the weather conditions. William Husk certainly does love his coffee, he thought to himself.

X

On his third visit to William, the old man did not come to meet the delivery driver, but left a scrawled note pinned to the front door. It said:

Keep your distance! Put my grocery box in the coal bunker to your left, but <u>only</u> after you have checked it is all there. I ordered -

It was not unusual - these days - for customers to prefer not to come to the door. The delivery driver was happy to oblige the old man, and happy also that the old man seemed to trust him enough to audit the contents of his grocery box. It felt like the beginning of a new era in their customer service relationship, though he hoped at least they might meet again soon at the front door.

IX

"Feckless! And idle! A layabout too, I don't doubt it." On the fourth delivery to the riverbank cottage, William Husk had come to the door again to receive his goods, on account that the last time he had delivered, the delivery driver had put the grocery box in the compost bin and not the coal bunker as instructed. He was to be scolded for his inattention to detail. The driver smiled and apologised, sincerely.

On the fifth delivery the old man checked his groceries and surprised the driver with a glimmer of excitement as he counted out his supplies. He chuckled to himself and the driver almost fancied a half smile was sent in his direction.

VII

Another note was pinned to the door on the sixth occasion that the delivery driver came to the cottage. He checked the goods and made sure to place them in the coal bunker, and not the compost bin.

The same note was there on the seventh visit and it had not been moved, giving the driver a little cause for concern. In the coal bunker he found the previous visit's order, untouched. Concerned, he knocked on the door of the cottage, but there was no reply. He looked through various windows, but could see no evidence that the old man was about. When he arrived back at the depot after his delivery round, he followed protocol and reported a safeguarding concern to his supervisor.

This being a tale of good will, we make the imaginative leap that it was a time of some nostalgic past or a more socially-concerned alternative present, when a civic department would mobilise toward the wellbeing of a valued senior citizen of the community, and immediately send a well-dressed, kind and concerned official by the name of Pete to the grubby old door of the riverbank cottage, to check on the welfare of William Husk.

V

"You nosey bastard! You blithering idiot… you bloody feckless idle gossiping layabout!"

The old man was not best pleased with the delivery driver and was not short of commentary on the situation the next time he came with the grocery box. For his part, the driver was just delighted to have his old misery back at the cottage and on top form. Directing matters from his doorstep, William had him call out from behind his mask the contents of the order before putting them in the coal bunker and then, in William's words, pissing off.

"And next time you come, don't think I will have forgotten what you did!"

At least then, there would still be a next time.

III

There followed a resumption of the new normal, to coin a phrase of the day, in which the delivery driver was favoured with an appearance at the door of the riverbank cottage by old man William Husk, with directions on unloading and checking the goods of his grocery box and the occasional insult which wavered between almost-friendly and, sometimes, a little half-hearted. There was no mention of 'what you did' but whether the old man had forgotten, the driver could not tell. He did seem to be consuming an awful lot of coffee.

II

It would perhaps have been about the eleventh time the delivery driver went out to the riverbank cottage to find a note from William tacked to the door which read:

Moved on the weekend. Redirect to Fallow Pastures. Don't be late.

Some investigative work on the telephone with his supervisor led, at the end of his regular round, to a retirement home in town. They weren't letting anyone on the premises but pointed to a south-facing window overlooking an ancient yew on the pleasantly manicured grounds. Other people were visiting other windows, the delivery driver noted. He took the grocery box to the window indicated, and there was William, on the other side, annoyed. He shouted about the time, about the delay, about how long he had waited. It was very faint through triple-glazed windows that apparently didn't open, and the driver could only barely make out the traditional insult. The old man signalled to the package and the driver picked out each item to demonstrate all was in good order. Uncertain where to leave it, with the old man cursing impatiently, he indicated he would take it to reception where he left it with a nurse standing almost to attention on security detail.

There were no more orders from William Husk.

I

The delivery driver missed his visits to the riverbank cottage and there came a time when an order from a new customer took him close by Fallow Pastures, so he looked in for the old man. Again restrictions prevented him from going in or having a useful conversation with anyone in charge, and it was with no small regret that he found the window with a view of the yew tree, and there looked in upon an empty room.

As Day Follows Night

"As a young man I never lost a moment's sleep concerning myself with waking up in the dark," he once said to me, by way of introduction, "I was as sure as anyone that the next day would follow in due course."

Of all the lies Galloway ever told - and he told many - perhaps the one I admire the most is his audacious assertion that neither the dusk nor the dawn, and by extension neither night nor day, are absolute or assured in the experience of human kind. You perhaps suppose he meant that each sunrise should be a blessing and each sunset a blessed relief? I too assumed as much as I heard him speak it the first time, but then of course I did not know what a gifted and prodigious liar he was; nor did I realise he was rehearsing upon me his latest skit; nor could I know, having just recently made his acquaintance, that Galloway was an unpretentious teller of tall tales - if such a thing is not a contradiction of states - and that his lies were so much more digestible for lack of metaphor; and I was yet to learn that the art of true deception is the interwoven tapestry of truth and fiction so finely needled that to stand back and admire it one might be overwhelmed with the simple beauty of its apparent veracity and not see - amidst the harmonies it writes upon one's instincts - the fine threads of enchantment and misdirection that hold such visions in place.

"I recall a time when the sun set on a Tuesday, early afternoon, and didn't rise again until well after Lent," - thus introduced to me, he sipped his pint and set it upon the bar, and launched into the recounting of his long days in the Arctic Circle.

"I saw such things… such lingering days… such relentless nights… but I never imagined a day that just wouldn't come. It's no certain thing, the day. No certain thing at all."

"Well what do you mean," I wondered, presuming this a reference to the Scandinavian condition of melancholia under the long twilight of the north. But, as I've already said, this was no allegory on his part - a particular Wednesday morning, some years ago on the island of Grímsey in the Arctic Circle, had failed to arrive and after a long and uncertain wait a Thursday finally dawned to the relief of all. Galloway made a lengthy evocation of his purpose on Grímsey - his occupations, his accommodations, the food he consumed, the comfort of his bed and his writing desk, his routines and timekeeping, the weather, the coming and going of ferries to Horn and Reykjavík, the bleakness of flora and fauna, the lack of birds, the various qualities of various mosses, the hospitality of locals, the complexities of Icelandic grammar and all manner of other details to colour the descriptions of passing time in the Arctic before the day that did not come, and then, the days after it. Of the Wednesday that did not arrive, he found himself short on detail, and yet was most insistent nonetheless.

"I believe the new day was a Thursday... perhaps Friday... no no, Thursday, yes, Thursday," he asserted uncertainly, "but certainly, I am sure of it, there was a Wednesday that never came. And if it wasn't a Wednesday, so what? We missed one day in Grímsey, upon my soul no doubt about that."

"Missing a day and a day going missing are two quite different things," I said and we fell into a discussion about drunkenness and veisalgia and narcotics and narcolepsy and insomnia and amnesia and the many reasons why a man should think that a day had been lost when in fact it most likely the man himself had been lost.

Galloway would not concede however, being sure of both his health and his clarity of thinking at the time; he next described the data, denouements and proceeds of his long years since Grímsey engaged in the practical observation of linear time for fear that his days were numbered intermittently. He had apparently amassed a wealth of anecdotal evidence on the matter and seemed limitlessly generous in disseminating his conclusions that evening at the bar. I will not say that he was not entertaining, for he was; and his evidence was both comprehensive and compelling. But for all that, I had no feeling for this phenomena and I could not bring myself to accept it. His grand deceit - as I now know it - was foundering.

"What were you about last week, on Thursday," he asked me, suddenly, "where did you go and what did you do?"

A master liar of Galloway's standing may tack close to the wind and skirt the rocky shallows, risking all, yet still have about them a stroke or two of mastery to bring home the bounty of their fantastical voyage. Here then heaves toward port the captain of the rotten ship Beguiler to land his mendacious cargo.

"Well of course I was at work... no, wait, not work, I had a long weekend of leave... so I must've had a lazy day at home... I went to the town market for cheese, that's right!"

"Town market's Friday," said the barmaid, helpfully. The evening was slow and she'd enjoyed Galloway's recounting of his adventure in the Arctic Circle whilst buffing glasses and pulling the odd leisurely stout for the bar's only other customer, an old farm hand perched at the far end of the long counter.

"Yes, you're right, Friday. Then... let me think... Thursday... did I go to the allotments?"

"Did you?" wondered Galloway, "did you do your house chores? Did you visit the library or the museum or the theatre? Did you refuel the car or service the bicycle? Did you visit a neighbour or go for a long walk or read a book or even a chapter of a book or a newspaper or magazine or did you go for coffee or watch a film? Did you breakfast in town, or lunch in town, or dine in town for tea or dinner? Did you meet friends or phone them, did you write a letter or a postcard or a list of important things or a cheque or a nonsensical story about soup or frogs or sailors or the meaning of temporality or the evolution of eyes as a proof of God? Did you come to the pub? - "

"He didn't come to the pub," interrupted the barmaid.

"Are you sure he didn't? Were you here?"

"I was definitely here," she confirmed, after checking last week's rota on the staff noticeboard, "though come to think of it, I can't remember the shift. I can't remember him being here anyway, or you for that matter."

"Who was here?" pressed Galloway.

"I expect he was," she said, thumbing over her shoulder at the old farm hand, the pub's most devout regular.

"I don't remember," called out the old man.

"No, nor do I, come to think of it," said the barmaid.

"Does anyone remember last Thursday?" asked the master liar.

Does anyone remember last Thursday? I certainly couldn't. Galloway shook his head slowly, took a draught of his pint, and concluded mournfully, "another one gone missing then."

Deterge

"All this?" asked the man in the brown overalls.

All this, an inventory: a chaise longue, a Pembroke table, Shaker cabinets and chests of drawers, a suite of Chesterfields, Victorian armchairs garishly reupholstered, sideboards, a rolltop bureau, a coffer, dresser, wardrobe, armoire, bath chair, Farthingale chair, ladderback chair, iron bed in the Art Nouveau style, divan, trundle bed, candlestands, dressing table, Cumbernauld table, highboy, lowboy, rustic styles and mission styles and arts and craft styles; mirrors - in the bathroom, the second bedroom, at the bottom of the stairs (full-length) by the front door, a small one in the shape of a crucifix, copper framed, hooked by a string to the inside of the door to the cupboard under the stairs; candlesticks, lamps, bookends, figurines, pots, pans, placemats, tumblers, paperweights, picture frames (the children and his wife under the mile-marker post at Land's End one summer's holiday, his wife - he only ever called her 'Chick' - in a studio portrait in her Land Army uniform, Chick in her scarf on a blustery day, Chick and he outside the church on the day they renewed their wedding vows, Chick and their eldest in his first suit on the day he started at the bank, Chick, Chick, Chick in frames all around the house), brass instruments and Bakelite devices retired to display pieces, one thousand objects gathering dust on mantelpieces and shelves and in drums, tins, boxes, jars, bottles, buckets, cases, crates and chests; mementos of the lives of the children - exercise books, library cards, drawings, letters, poems, merit badges, school reports and school ties, spelling certificates, swimming certificates, athletics certificates, a Geoff Hurst Football School Merit Award (was that even me, I don't remember it), first watches, baby shoes, hospital bracelets - though not my pickled appendix in a jar - birthday cards and sundry trinkets; trinkets; a life, lives, recalled in trinkets; his medals, multiple, from the wars, plural, of which he never spoke; his tools, his tins of ironmongery, batteries new and used, sizes various; a collection of Dutch pin badges, a heavy drawer of mismatched cutlery both silver (tarnished) and steel (stainless and dull); pottery and crockery acquired ad-hoc and piecemeal over a lifetime rather than collected by intent; old calculators in crowded boxes and cupboards and sideboards, seemingly one for every room of the house; journals, digests, quarterlies, monthlies, weeklies, pamphlets, chapbooks, magazines, editions, notices and newsletters; paperwork everywhere and notebooks full of the trivia of the monotonous interstices of existence - shopping lists, to-do lists, dates with their significance left unstated, telephone numbers, totting up and short divisions, measurements, sums of money (a few pounds or less), book titles, words alone without context, partial words from solitary games of Hangman, anagrammatical rearrangements and fragmented evidence of other guessing games played on paper; pens and pencils ubiquitous; a small eclectic collection of well-used paperbacks, some with broken spines and loose leaves, including Walser, Footman, and an English language copy of Péguy's long form Portal To The Mystery Of Hope; a rusty old Paschley Royal Mail bicycle leaning against the outside of the terraced house, chained with an old heavy chain and locked with an old heavy padlock, the keys... somewhere; a white panel van on the street outside, at the gate, shutter up, radio on and transfers along back and side panels: T. Poes & Associates, House Clearances.

"All of it," I said, "take everything."

"Nothing you'd want to keep - for sentimental reasons," he checked, and eyeing the wallet I produced from my pocket, "that'll be £300, for cash, Sir."

"I'll just keep the receipt," I said, as he wrote it out, "for my records."

Muttonhead

"We'll be off to the ferry then," called Mother Bidna to the old man.

Two of her elder boys were hauling the studded leather carcass of the old Chesterfield down the hill of The Terrace, a narrow rough cobbled shutt of cottages, eager to get a start.

"Storm's coming up," the old man shouted through the house to Bidna, who was standing on the doorstep of Number One at the top of the steep terrace, with the rest of her children engaged in the act of waiting solemnly for mother's orders.

"He knows the weather now!" Bidna winked at her brood.

"Cushions?" Two of her girls held up the old leather squares.

"Coin?" Her other son presented her purse for inspection.

"Prudence?" The oldest girl stepped forward, a young teen with a babe in a sling across her front, and patted her on the head.

"And I've got the victuals," she said, hoisting a large canvas tote onto her shoulder, "so we'd better get after them boys."

She called back to the old man. "Ninnyhammer!"

The children called out their own choice pejoratives - "rum codger!"; "lubbock!"; "swiver!" That sort of thing.

"Feckless idle layabout!" chimed Hedren, the daughter with her younger sister in a sling.

This latter elicited a firm response from the old man out the back of the house, though he didn't come out from wherever he was busy idling - "Oi! There's no need for that!

Mind your bloody language you!"

The troupe departed, following the boys down the hill. "What an inveterate loafer. Nevertheless," said Bidna to Hedren, "your language was surprisingly sharp. Don't you go repeating that in front of the young ones."

At the bottom of the cobbled hill The Terrace took a sharp left to loop around the chandlery, and the young handsome mechanic loitered at the entrance to his yard. "The Expeditionary Force! Where are you all off to then?"

"Up to the Ferry," said Bidna.

"In this weather?" It was perfectly fine, in fact, though quite still and a little humid. "Storm's coming up, you know."

"Everyone's the meteorologist today, aren't they?"

Kitto and Wooda, the elder boys, had reached the quay on their steady march and were afforded time for a quick rest while the family caught up. They were sitting each on one arm of their cargo watching fishermen coming in with their catches.

"Andy says storm's coming up," reported Kitto to his mother.

"Does he now? Best we get on then, wouldn't want to be caught short before the ferry."

The elder boys hefted the sofa and pressed on toward the lifeboat station and the shore path. The family followed, Bidna bringing up the rear, serenaded by gulls agitated and expectant at the coming in of the fishing boats.

"There'll be no ferry in these conditions," said the commander of the lifeboat station, after engaging with the passing convoy of Bidna and children, and hearing of her plans. It was still perfectly fine weather, no chill on the air and no hint of a breeze. "We're getting ready for a busy shift, what with this storm coming up. If you want my advice, - "

Bidna was not inclined to take his advice, all things considered. The family marched across the buttress of the tide wall and onto the rougher ground of the shore path, labouring up rough-hewn stairways and over wooden styes, Kitto and Wooda sometimes needing the assistance of their younger brother at the most difficult obstacles. The sun continued to shine moderately in a clear sky, and the wind declined to blow.

At midday they took lunch in the shade of a wind-twisted white poplar tree, assembling the old blue Chesterfield and taking turns enjoying its cracked and weathered comforts. Bidna and Hedren quietly contemplated the wide estuary beyond the shore path, the dunes and the piles of grey-white boulders; Kitto and Wooda stretched out on the grass to rest, and the other siblings took turns entertaining their youngest sister, Prudence.

Mother Bidna eventually called time on festivities, they packed up their picnic, stripped the Chesterfield, and the boys once more took up the frame of the old studded sofa. They trudged on at a leisurely pace toward the ferry; the afternoon was hot and still, the going easy. Gulls called to them, barely moving on languid thermals, and in the distance, as they rounded the promontory, they could see no ferry though the sky was clear and bright. Mounting the stile over on to the ferry lane, manhandling their furniture and grouping together for the final trudge down to the pier, they intermittently scanned the water for signs of their transport, and then along the opposite shore promenade and their destination. Nobody spoke. They descended down the gentle slope of the lane and came to a sullen halt at the empty pier.

"No ferry then," said Kitto.

Mother Bidna scanned the skies for this incoming storm that had waylaid their planned excursion, but all was fine and clear. The ticket hut was closed and boarded up with the sign,

No Ferry's Tday

"Muttonhead," she grumbled, displeased with the apostrophe as much as the circumstance.

The elder boys carried the sofa to the end of the pier, and the family set it up looking outward across the water, so that they might catch an early sight of the ferry, should it materialise in the eye of a storm that didn't seem to be coming. They took turns on the watch through the long late afternoon, the children happily amusing themselves on the pier, under the pier, behind the sofa, in the mud, in the shallows, in the empty car park, on the roof of the ticket hut, up and down the ferry lane (though strictly within ear-shot), along the grassy dunes of the strand, on the smooth round rocks of the tide wall and around the skirts of the mother Bidna to her passing amusement and then impatience and then amusement again. As evening threatened, a dog-walker from the ferry lane helpfully called out that there would be no ferries today, on account of the coming storm. Bidna did not answer him, and after hesitating for the longest time, he shrugged and pressed on with his own occupation.

"Muttonhead," she said quietly in his direction, though it surely was not his fault.

I Could've Killed You Back There

In the late autumn I found a Tortoiseshell butterfly on the wall in the spare room. I read - in Sebald, I think - that they just look for somewhere to wait, and then don't move again, and die, as if that was what they were waiting for all along. This one wasn't moving so I figured maybe it was dead already, but I didn't vacuum it up straightaway, just in case. I forgot about it for a while and maybe a week later there it was again, on the wall, only in a different spot. I looked closely and it didn't seem to be moving, but I thought, no, you can't tell, so leave it for a while. And when I looked again, it was gone.

A few days later I just avoided crushing it in the jamb of the bedroom door. It might've been dead anyway, for all I could see, as it still looked immobile to me. Alright then, I thought, better just let it be. Maybe it hasn't found the right place yet to wait for death. Over the next month, though I never saw a flicker of movement, it kept reappearing in new places. One time it was on the floor and I didn't want to touch it, in case I damaged it or worse - so I made a mental note of its position to make sure I didn't step on it, and promised to keep an eye on it. I forgot of course, and was only reminded when I found it somewhere else. I could've killed you back there, I thought.

When I found it in the void between the window pane and the cheap, broken secondary glazing that is jammed closed, and it was by now the beginning of December, and it had a train of cobweb and dust attached to it from somehow crawling into the window void, I thought it was done for. That thing will be frozen at the next frost and stuck in there forever, I thought, near to the curled up remains of a dead wasp I can't remove either, on account of the jammed plastic insulation. And then it was gone again, like some miraculous escape artist.

I discovered it in January at the top of the stairs, and its train of cobweb and dust was longer. I tried to get the detritus off with tweezers but it wasn't coming loose and the butterfly seemed to be getting about just fine anyway with a collection of grit and hair and dust like a miniature backpack of keepsakes. Next time I saw it, it was on the wall at the bottom of the stairs, then on the opposite wall, then back up near the top again. In between, it disappeared somewhere, only to collect more rubbish in its wake.

This went on well into the spring. I never once saw it move even a single cotton thread of antenna - whenever I inspected it closely, it played dead. Dead and waiting. But the whole time it was marching about the house imperceptibly slowly. Each time I rediscovered it was like bumping into an old friend. I told my girlfriend about it when she visited the house, and she said, I think it's the spirit of your mother.

She was always saying things like that.

In the early summer I found it tipped over on the floor of the landing. Pretty sure it's dead now, I thought. I picked it up and put it in a plant pot under a spider plant, and it is still there - finally, death had taken it. I wasn't sad - it was an insect - but I was kind of sorry, so I bought a print of a tortoiseshell butterfly in its memory, and had it framed, and hung it up over the bed where I had once seen it on its journey back from the broken window void.

When my girlfriend came round, she said "I'm not sleeping under that, it's like having your mother in the room, watching us in bed."

She asked me, "what were you thinking - it's weird".

Colloquium

Prologue

"Oh don't you worry about all that, it's just his little joke," explained Nash, concerning the incident in reception, "you'll get used to it - there's always one! Anyway, welcome the Annual Universal Undo Conference - your first time!"

Months had passed since Creed's initial transgression that brought him into contact with these peculiar people and their infuriating obsession with fixing things in the proper manner. They still hadn't fixed things for him, really.

Nash *had* rescued him from the little joker on the front desk mind you:

"I'm looking for Universal Undo," Creed had asked him.

"The what, Sir?" wondered the little joker.

"Universal Undo? The conference?"

"Not here, Sir."

"There must be some mistake, this is the Imperial Hotel isn't it?"

"It is yes,"

"Then it says right here, on the invitation…"

"Ah, that was last week sir - the date, here, see?"

"But that's today's date."

"You are quite right sir, one moment… here we are - they are in the Circle Suite, along the corridor to your left."

"You didn't know that already?"

"My mistake sir - we all make them, don't we. As you'll know."

"What do you mean by that?"

"The conference, sir - Universal Undo? In the Circle Suite. You're attending? Leastways you have an invitation, so you must be familiar with mistakes."

The back and forth was interrupted by Nash, who called his colleague over toward the Circle Suite, along the corridor to Creed's left. As Creed approached his mentor, relieved and a touch confused, he took a glance back at the little joker on reception.

"Oh, don't you worry about all that," explained Nash.

They had barely stepped a foot into the large auditorium of the Circle Suite when Creed took a sharp intake of breath. "Blimey, Nash - look!" he exclaimed in a hushed tone, pointing across the room to where a small gathering of attendees were making pre-conference small talk, "Over there!"

Nash frowned.

"There look! Talking with Durgan and Skipp, do you see?"

Nash frowned again.

"Dammit man, it's Cove! Eustace Cove! Of all the… Cove is here. He's wearing a moustache, but it's him alright. What the devil?"

Nash frowned more. "I don't see him. Are you sure? It can't be."

"What is he up to? Coming here? This is no good, Nash. This is no good at all!"

First Meeting

"Welcome to the Corrective Measures Forum," said the host, "you must be Creed?"

It wasn't an unfriendly tone, though Creed was struck by the rather autocratic presumption of using neither given name nor title in the greeting. Then again, he supposed he was here as a sort of punishment, or at least, to make amends for a transgression. Perhaps they didn't give you your title back until you'd proved your re-education was satisfactory, by their assessment. By this man's assessment.

"Whealcoates," said the host, by way of introduction, offering a friendly hand. "Please, do grab yourself tea and a biscuit. The government don't pay for that of course, but we like to facilitate a comfortable working environment for our guests - a few refreshments go a long way!"

As Creed poured a cup of tea, Whealcoates explained the process for the day.

"We'll start with a sharing - you know, what happened, why it happened, why you came here today to tell us all about it, and what you hope to achieve from the meeting. I'll manage the running order, and give you the nod when it's your turn. After all the presentations are finished, we'll invite group feedback, and see where it goes from there. It's a very fluid process. Not many in today, so we'll have time for some very solid work, I should think."

Indeed, after Creed and the host Whealcoates, there was only one other attendee for Corrective Measures. Hardly a forum.

The room was arranged with two rows of chairs in a rather large circle, perhaps with fifteen chairs in the front row, and another twenty five or so in the second. Encouraged by Whealcoates, Creed placed himself in the front row, and if the host, sitting in the second row, was at twelve o'clock, then Creed was at about a quarter to ten. The other attendee, a young professional-looking woman, was also in the second row, at about half past five. She looked very serious.

"Are we ready?" asked Whealcoates, at no-one in particular. The woman nodded, and Creed followed suit, instinctively.

"Then we begin," said the host.

There was a long pause. A very long pause.

Creed wondered if he had been expected to start, though he was quite sure Whealcoates had said he would be given a cue. Was that the cue? It didn't seem to have been aimed in his direction. He looked at the woman. She was unmoved.

He turned to look at Whealcoates. "Shall I start?"

The host signalled silently for him to wait.

The pause continued for quite some time. Creed wondered if this was a contemplative moment. Alright then, he decided, let me get my thoughts in order -

"Would you care to open the meeting, Creed?" said Whealcoates. Was that a cue to tell his story?

"You want me to begin?"

"When you are ready, yes. You know - the whens, the whats and the whys… as we discussed earlier. In your own words."

"Well, my name is Professor Chri - "

"Just surnames, if you don't mind," said Whealcoates.

So that was a definite thing then, thought Creed.

Creed

I can't honestly say I was paying much attention at the date and time in question. Indeed, if the details of it hadn't been laid out in the official notification, I don't think I would ever have known I was in the wrong. I don't mean to pretend to ignorance or innocence or some kind of superiority, but honestly, I am not a raving idiot that goes screeching about the place. I don't suffer from rage or maniacal attention-seeking and I am rarely in a rush for anything. So I was entirely surprised to hear I had been captured by a speeding camera at six miles per hour over the speed limit in a built-up area on the Underpass. To tell the truth - and why not, since I'm here? - I didn't know there was a camera on the underpass, and I don't suppose I knew the speed limit either although of course I've since seen that it is well sign-posted. Anyway I don't mean for this to sound like I'm suspicious of the notification, although there is no credible way for me to disprove it, and I chose to come here today not to whine about the situation but, being perfectly honest with you, to avoid the endorsement on my licence and the automatic fine that goes with it. I'm not a miserly fellow by any means but the thought of paying for something I may or may not have done - oh I know for all intents and purposes, in the context of this meeting, I have admitted the guilt of it by my very attendance... anyway, I suppose I was rather hoping that if I came here and allowed you to remind me of the highway code, and appeared contrite - not in a false way - and proved I have a better understanding of the speed limits of this town and the expectations of the law, and assured everyone - genuinely - that I would pay better attention to the signs and to my speedometer, I might avoid an unnecessary expense of a road traffic violation statutory fine. Which is what it said in the notification letter - that I could take the fine and the endorsement on my licence, or come here, listen to you chaps, prove my road-worthiness, and, for want of a better way of putting it, get away without having to pay the fine. Although, of course, I have paid for my place here at the Corrective Measures Forum and it more or less costs the same as the fine, but I'll not bemoan it. Better to look willing, I suppose, than churlish. And at least I got free tea and biscuits. Or biscuit, to be precise, not that I'm counting.

"Thank you Creed, a very interesting first contribution. I'm sure there is plenty to think about there. Shall we take a moment?" Whealcoates introduced another of his uncomfortably long silences.

I wonder if I went too far, thought Creed. After all -

"Porter? Would you care to follow on?" asked the host eventually, of the woman at half past five in the seating arrangement.

Porter

It was at my good friend's wedding that I first had the idea for the *Vibia* app; you probably won't have heard of it because it didn't get past beta stage testing, which I abandoned last week when I decided to come here to talk about how my algorithms have ruined everything. Well not everything of course. I should probably not be so emotional. Anyway, at this wedding I thought, wow, I made this happen. I mean, I didn't organise the wedding. But I introduced the happy couple. So I started thinking about how I did that - because it was a fairly unique situation, you see - and how maybe I could make a living doing that. I had met Tessula - that was the bride - when we shared accommodation at University. I was studying at the business school; I had just finished my masters when Tess got married to Reuben - that was the groom, obviously, whom I knew from home - and I thought, I could make an app for people like Tess and Ben - you know, people with specific challenges in romance and… all that. Anyway, to cut a very long story short, we got to beta testing by and by, with millions of hours work and some very generous venture capital, and I thought we had a brilliant piece of software - I say we, meaning Heartfelt Inc., my company - which we wanted to try out on a small control group before taking to public launch. That's where everything went wrong, you see. That's why I'm here. Oh poor Irena! (She's another friend). What have I done?

(Creed was wondering whether he had come to the wrong session, or whether Porter had. But she seemed so certain of her place here, Creed thought, whilst he had been wrong-footed from the very start. He glanced at Whealcoates who appeared fully absorbed in the story, and not the slightest bit concerned that Porter was off-topic. The more he considered, the more he was certain he had come to the wrong meeting - there had never been any specific mention here of the Driving & Vehicles Licensing Agency, who, after all, had offered him the chance to re-educate himself on the Highway Code. And what was this story of Porter's now, was she making it up as she went along?)

Vibia just got it all so wrong. Irena followed the app's advice and rejected a proposal from Leo whilst she went in pursuit of someone called Saul who wasn't even supposed to be testing the beta stage. But somehow - and we still aren't entirely sure why - the data profiles matched precisely between Irena and Saul. If only I hadn't used friends and mutual acquaintances to test the damned thing - what with all the other specifics around their dating challenges. Now Leo is suing me, Saul is stalking me - I wouldn't be surprised if he's outside right now - and Irena won't answer my calls or even log in to the app. It is a complete and utter omnishambles. (I may have changed some names for data protection purposes.)

"I do apologise," said Creed, to no-one in particular and to the room, after Porter had finished, "I have clearly come to the wrong meeting. I'm supposed to be doing a driver's refresher course after the, um, well, the aforementioned road traffic offence. I did not mean to trivialise the… whatever it is you are doing here. Entirely my mistake, of course."

Whealcoates was quick to point out that in his attempt to admit a mistake in such gracious and sincere fashion, Creed had at the very least modelled the perfect process for moving forward with Corrective Measures. But as he was about to find out (so Whealcoates continued) his attendance here was no mistake.

Feedback

'How did we do?'

An email from the Driving & Vehicles Licensing Agency received the following day outlined Creed's progress on the restorative education course in pursuit of avoiding an endorsement on his licence, advised potential dates for a second meeting which promised to bring Creed much closer to his goal, and included a link to an online feedback form. The progress statement was vague enough and the date options so unclear that Creed had no idea how many more sessions he would have to attend and certainly no clue as to what he was expected to learn from the process, other than that he was sorry - very sorry indeed - for not paying attention to the speed limit on the Underpass. He meant to express all this on the feedback link provided in the email, but found, unsurprisingly, that the survey wasn't very user-friendly, asked all the wrong questions and only allowed for answers from a selection of largely homogenised statements thought up by a civil servant who clearly had never been to a Corrective Measures Forum, or didn't really care what Creed thought about it.

He could still give full rein to his bemusement with the final, open question - Any Other Comments - and did so:

There doesn't seem to be anywhere else to adequately express my confusion about the re-education session I attended or my disappointment in knowing I haven't yet completed the process. I cannot see where this is going or what I need to achieve in order to satisfy the DVLA of my competence adequately enough to avoid the looming fine and endorsement on my licence. Where to begin? Firstly, I suppose, I must express some shock and disappointment that my case seems to have been handed over to an amiable but intolerably tolerant official, Whealcoates, who allowed the first meeting to veer so wildly off course that we became no more than a collection of confessors at Quaker meeting, or what I understand of one anyway. After listening to preposterous stories of various uncategorised mistakes, misinterpretations and misunderstandings - my own being the only one that actually involved a road traffic offence - we then had to endure several hours of |

Here Creed ran up against the web survey character count limiter and the form refused to accept any more of his constructive feedback, or to let him click back to edit his Any Other Comment. Satisfied he had at least made a point with the general tone of his entry, he hit the SUBMIT button.

Nothing happened.

Against his better instinct and knowing he was only making things worse, he tried the rapid multi-click approach to wake the website up. It didn't work. Eventually the spinning wheel icon simply froze. He tried entering the page again via his email link, but that no longer worked either. He made a mental note to add that to the feedback next time around, if there was to be such a thing: he wasn't even sure if he had managed to book a date for his second meeting.

He telephoned the Driving & Vehicles Licensing Agency helpline for further assistance, but got lost in a maze of automated options and dialled himself into a dead end. He was making another mental note to add the failure of the telephone system to his list of mental notes on the general failures of the Driving & Vehicles Licensing Agency when the Aureleians knocked at his front door.

The Aureleians

"Hello my name is Anita - "

"And I'm Will," interjected Will.

"We're from the Aureleian Society," continued Anita, "have you heard of the Aureleians or our work?"

Anita and Will looked like the sort of trouble that any doorstep proselytes might bring to the day. They must have known that was what Creed was thinking. He could tell his face was broadcasting its own sermon, which involved impolite instructions for ending shared spiritual experiences.

"Oh we aren't here to tell you the error of your ways or anything like that," said Anita.

"We just want to help," added Will, "you know, if there is anything you're a bit stuck with, or something where an extra pair of brains might be useful, a different perspective... that sort of thing."

This was a new way to put people off balance, thought Creed. He couldn't immediately come up with any adequate deflection, so fell back on an old, tried and tested favourite.

"Look you're wasting your time here I'm afraid. I'm a committed non-believer. I'm not interested in irrational debates, sorry. You'll have more luck at 11A."

There wasn't an 11A on the street but it should take them a while to figure it out. He went to close the door.

"There must be some misunderstanding," said Anita, verbally putting a metaphorical foot in the door, "The Aureleian Society isn't a religious order. Far from it. Quite the opposite, in fact."

"Wholly rational, by definition" said Will, "real-world solutions, without the supernatural, so to speak."

Creed was confused and just a little curious, but at the same time - "That's fascinating I'm sure, but I just don't have the time right now. Good luck on your mission, or whatever it is."

"At least take a card," instructed Anita, as Will held out printed details of how to get in touch with The Aureleian Society, "There's always someone on the line, and you'll never get diverted into a dead-end with The Aureleians, you know."

Arrested by this last comment, and instinctively obeying Anita's instruction, Creed took the card.

"I'm not suicidal or anything," he said.

"Of course not," said Anita.

"And there's always The Samaritans for that," added Will.

"We're here for the more tangible problems," explained Anita, edging closer to the door, which Creed was failing to close.

"Making sure you get what you need in life," said Will, "to keep moving forward. Call us, any time, or we can have a cup of tea now if you like, and see if we can help you with that knotty problem that is driving you up the wall?"

"What knotty problem?" asked Creed, moving to block Anita who took a subtle step back.

"Any knotty problem," she said, "any knotty problem at all. We're here to unravel for you, and straighten things out."

"I'll give you a call then," said Creed, waving the business card. He closed the door.

Outside, Anita bent down to the letter box and pushed it open. "We'll wait on your call then," she said through the hole in the door.

Creed half expected them to remain standing there until he had called the number on the card, but after a brief pause, they turned and left. He moved to a street-facing window to see where they would go next, but they seemed to have disappeared already. Not making house-to-house visits then.

An unremarkable car passed by the house, the windows dark, but it seemed to Creed that it might be The Aureleians leaving the scene. A moment later a similar car, parked a short way up the street, started up and pulled away, following the first. And then a third car, of equally similar nondescript features, arrived outside Creed's driveway from the opposite direction. By the standards of this quiet residential street, it was quite the rush hour. Now who was this?

Northcott-Cornish

"I've come about the feedback you left with the DVLA," said Northcott-Cornish, after introducing herself as 'a customer satisfaction handler' for Colloquium, private contractors to the government who ran the Corrective Measures Forums.

"May I?" she asked, indicating she would like entry into his home.

Creed was astonished by the speed of the response from his internet feedback survey, which he wasn't even sure had worked when he submitted it, not half an hour previously. He let her across the threshold he had only just successfully defended from The Aureleians.

They discussed his driving licence.

"I wanted to avoid a fine, yes," admitted Creed, "but now I'm wondering if the whole thing has been a waste of time and perhaps I should've just paid it and taken the hit."

Northcott-Cornish wanted to reassure him he was on the path to a full clean licence, that his fine would be revoked, and that if he could just be patient with the programme, he would undoubtedly reap rewards that even she could not predict in the moment.

"I don't want to come across excessively hyperbolic, but it might change the course of your life," she speculated. That was rather grandiose, thought Creed.

"Will you just try another meeting?" asked the customer satisfaction handler.

"Alright" said Creed.

If he had hoped to placate her by acquiescing so meekly, and getting rid of her as quickly as possible, he was mistaken.

"Do you have any questions for me?" she asked him.

"I don't think so, no."

Are we done here? - thought Creed; can you go now? Will you let me alone? Shall we call it a day? Don't you have more important places to be?

Apparently, Northcott-Cornish did not have anywhere more important to be right then and there, other than ensuring that Creed really would attend another meeting. She wouldn't be sold on such an obvious ruse as Creed immediately agreeing without further question, so she set about answering the questions she assumed he had, even though he hadn't asked them. Creed only half listened. It was clear to him that as a private contractor, Colloquium not only placed a high value on the success rates of their contracts, but actually financially depended on preventing drop-outs from their programmes.

"In short," concluded Northcott-Cornish, "we care about your success, and we want to see this through with you, to get you to where you want to be."

In short, thought Creed, their reputation - and income - depended upon his success. They probably got paid a fee for each pass. And then it occurred to him that they probably got paid per session too; and it likely wouldn't do to have him sail through too quickly either.

"I hope that clears everything up," she said.

"It certainly helps," said Creed, "I think I just have one more question, if you don't mind?"

If she did mind, Northcott-Cornish didn't show it. Her face did not move a millimetre: which, thought Creed, probably meant she did mind quite a bit.

"Not at all," she said.

"How many more meetings do I have to attend before this is all done?"

Second Meeting

"I'm Rigby," said Rigby, introducing herself to Creed.

"Are you running the meeting?" wondered Creed.

"Oh no, I'm a participant… I'm surprised we haven't met before - we've been doing this for a while, eh?"

"How long exactly have you been on the programme?" asked Creed.

At that point the Forum Facilitator drew the meeting to order. There were six or seven attendees this time. The facilitator was a different person, but the process was entirely familiar to the way Whealcoates ran his meetings.

There was a short period of silent contemplation.

"Barnard," said the facilitator, "perhaps you'll start us off."

Barnard's story concerned his falling out with his fishing club associates after an incident with an overly-aggressive pike during a tournament on the River Smite. He'd hooked a champion, he explained, only for it to pull free after an almighty struggle to land it. He'd fallen over in the process, flooded his waders, and let the thing get away, much to the amusement of his colleagues. And then - Barnard said - the beast had come back for more. To Creed it seemed an improbable but well-crafted story, and not altogether unfamiliar. The unfortunate fisherman explained that he had fallen out with club members over his obsession with the pike and the tall tales he told about the several attempts he had made to return to the Smite and reel in that beast, which he claimed was always waiting for him. It was 'sportsmanship unbecoming', said the club secretary. Members protested the story was beyond the acceptable limits of fisherman's tales. He had resigned his membership in a rage and had come to regret the whole thing.

While the forum observed a silent pause after Barnard's story, Creed turned to his near neighbour, Rigby, and whispered, "I still don't understand what this has got to do with road traffic offences."

"It's more of a multidisciplinary meeting really," said Rigby.

There were several more contributions before Creed was invited to speak, and certainly there was little to speak of involving the Highway Code. One woman had a mistranslation about the ownership of a bicycle during a trip to France, and that was just about as close to Creed's speeding offence as any of the stories got. Some were long and rambling, one was amusing, one tragic - the bicycle story - and one was startlingly pithy.

"I misunderstood the allegory in Rabelais" said Gates, a bookish young man. He sat down almost as soon as he stood up, looking inconsolable.

Creed was about to speak after his invitation from the facilitator when the meeting was interrupted. There was a commotion outside the meeting room - raised voices and some frantic knocking on a hard surface. The door to the meeting room was rattled but it had clearly been locked. The raised voice became a moderate yell, which subsided only by the apparent increase in its distance from the startled listeners of the Corrective Measures Forum as the yeller moved away. And then, on the other side of the meeting room close to the refreshment facilities, another door which Creed had hardly noticed and would have assumed the entrance to a larder or side room crashed open, and an angry man staggered in, unbalanced by his own effort to force a dramatic entry.

"Whealcoates!" said Creed.

Whealcoates

"Hello my name is Anita - "

"And I'm Will," interjected Will.

"We're from the Aureleian Society," continued Anita, "is now a good time?"

"Thank you for coming," Whealcoates said, and invited them in. He had been expecting them.

Anita and Will explained that they were there to listen, to attach no value judgments, and to help strategise for a new way of moving forward that would make him happy and ensure that he could continue to make good with the world. He was still, after all - said Anita - a decent person with a positive contribution to make. Whealcoates provided the tea and a biscuit.

He explained that of late he had found his work both stressful and unfulfilling, particularly in the light of poor client feedback. He had been temporarily reassigned away from the Corrective Measures Forum because his recent results were… "disappointing". Despite his training, he couldn't help but feel a sense of humiliation back at the office amongst his colleagues. There had been a time when he was proud to have posted regular wins from his forum work, to have been one of Colloquium's top field operators. He even won the company's Self Help Guru of The Year award back in oh-eight.

"If you were to imagine a timeline of recent notable events," asked Anita, "with a sequential bar chart of positive and negative occurrences - would you say it was a spiked profile with lots of peaks and troughs?"

Whealcoates paused to imagine his timeline of recent notable events. "Nice biscuit," said Will.

"Mostly flat," said Whealcoates, after giving it some thought.

"Well. As you'll know," said Anita, "that's quite a good start - "

" - with a steep-sided trough that continues to head in a downward direction into the present, and no noticeable upward shift further along the anticipated future timeline," added Whealcoates after further consideration, "making it, I suppose, a decline with no foreseeable levelling out. Not even a trough."

"That way lies despair," observed Will, putting down the remainder of his biscuit.

"Perhaps the timeline isn't the best model at this present point," said Anita, "let's take a look at the moment this recent dip began - was there a moment? An incident or... person? Try not to name names."

It seemed to start from a misunderstanding - Whealcoates explained - underpinned by the other's lack of trust in the process and even, perhaps, a little cynicism. ("Dear me, a cynic!" lamented Will, "A nihilist with a superiority complex.") Whealcoates described a man who came to a meeting - voluntarily! - but refused to engage in the process, demanded an instant result as if it were within the power of Whealcoates to change the history of the world, and submitted poor feedback when he couldn't get his way. But worse than that really, the company had failed to support him.

"Well, we are here to help now," said Anita, reassuring. She wanted to know more, and wanted Whealcoates to think more, about this person who seemed to be at the brink of his dramatic downward curve.

"You mean, who pushed me over the edge?" wondered Whealcoates.

"It is helpful to frame it less as a push or a trip," said Anita, "but rather as an accidental collision at a critical moment, probably as the result of distraction rather than outright intention."

"Like a pedestrian being bumped into the path of oncoming traffic by someone who was texting an important message on their phone," added Will, "unfortunate as it is, we as yet don't know what the text message was - it might be so important as to make the whole incident both explicable and forgivable."

Anita nodded. "Perhaps part of the strategy is to better understand the motives of the other person involved here, and in doing so - "

"Creed!" said Whealcoates.

Complaint

"He came out of nowhere; well, the pantry to be specific." Creed had not waited for the 'How did we do?' email to arrive from the Driving & Vehicles Licensing Agency to put in his complaint. He telephoned on the drive home from the meeting and would not be put off by the automated answering system.

"I don't know what you pay these Colloquium people to deliver your re-training courses," wondered Creed, "but it's an outrage that the tax-payer is footing the bill for these travesties. To be verbally attacked by a disgruntled facilitator for some negative feedback - and in such a threatening manner: he rattled - *rattled!* - the main doors to get in and positively yelled when he found them locked. But it didn't stop him. And do you know what he called me? Over some constructive criticism?!"

And so on and so forth.

"The least you can do is refund my training fee and waive the whole offence. I doubt you will, mind you. Who knows what backhanders have been given out to privatise these services, you'll just want to keep them coming. Well then, there you have it. That's how I've been treated today. I'll leave it up to the good people of the DVLA to sort it out. No doubt you'll send them round to harass me at my home about giving it another go. But I shall want to know what they are doing about this lunatic Whealcoates before I step one foot inside another of their Corrective Measures forums."

Et cetera.

As he arrived home he noted an overtly anonymous car parked on the street near his house - probably Northcott-

Cornish, he thought, laying in wait to smooth things over. But as he stepped up to his front door another nondescript vehicle pulled into his driveway - and that was Northcott-Cornish. She had someone else in the car with her.

That really did not take long at all, thought Creed.

"This is Nash," said Northcott-Cornish.

"I'm actually on the Corrective Measures programme like you,' said Nash, "a bit further along. Northcott-Cornish brought me here today to sort of help you out - a mentor, as it were. Someone who could guide you through the programme smoothly - and quickly, since Northcott-Cornish said you were keen to get this over with."

Nash seemed like a reasonable enough fellow.

After some overly-sincere apologies and the well-worn lines about striving to provide the very best service they possibly could, the customer satisfaction handler and Creed's new mentor tried to convince Creed to attend a third meeting.

They even almost - but not quite - promised it would be his final meeting before getting his speeding offence struck off.

"I shall want to know what you are doing about this lunatic Whealcoates before I step one foot inside another of your Corrective Measures forums" protested Creed. Northcott-Cornish assured him the errant facilitator was being dealt with.

"I think I just have one more question, if you don't mind?" said Creed, standing up now and looking out of his front window.

If she did mind, Northcott-Cornish didn't show it. "Not at all," she said.

"Who is that fellow over there in the car, up the street. One of yours?"

"Nothing to do with us," she said.

"Hmm," said Creed, thinking aloud.

Eustace Cove

"Who the devil are you and what is the meaning of this?" Creed had seen out his visitors from Colloquium after agreeing to one last attempt at a Corrective Measure, and immediately strode to the anonymous-looking car that was parked up nearby and had been, on and off, for the last few days. There was a waspish man at the wheel who was attempting to get his keys in the ignition to cut and run, but he had been surprised by Creed's swift approach and caught fumbling. Creed knocked petulantly on his window.

"What do you want? You're not from round here - are you spying on me? Come on, open up!"

Reluctantly, the unfortunate lurker wound down his window.

"Who are you?" demanded Creed.

"Eustace," said Eustace. "I'm here to help really - I don't mean to spy on you. I just wanted to make sure I had the right man before I made contact. I see you've been visited by Northcott-Cornish. Twice - that doesn't happen in a blue moon. They must be taking you seriously then."

"What are you talking about?"

Eustace Cove explained Colloquium, and Corrective Measures, and The Self-Help Desk, Technical Support Services, The Annual Universal Undo Conference, Solutions Trust, The Mutual Friendly Society of Stoics Anonymous and various other initiatives that Creed found difficult to keep track of. Or indeed, difficult to believe at all.

"That's plain ridiculous," Creed interjected.

The waspish man persisted, first confirming what Creed had already surmised, that Colloquium had a financial interest in maintaining his attendance at various meetings and training events for the sake of his driving licence. But he went on to describe a corporate empire of gigantic proportion notionally built to provide stable resolutions and long term answers to the world's problems; however, in practice - said Eustace - here was a demented civilising conspiracy quite entirely evangelistic about solution-based systems bent upon ironing out the smallest individual errors in pursuit of some wholly functional and correct utopia. Can you imagine? - said Eustace.

"Don't take my word for it. Go to Colloquium head office. Ask for Swales."

"Who is Swales?"

"There's no such person," said Eustace, and explained a ruse that would get him into the building.

"It all sounds entirely preposterous," said Creed, "I just want to avoid an endorsement on my driving licence. I think you should bugger off."

"Alright then," said Eustace, starting his car, "but if you change your mind, here is my card. Contact me if you decide to get out. They don't want to let you go, you know. There'll always be something needs fixing. I urge you to skip the next meeting, if you know what's good for you."

Third Meeting

There was a short period of silent contemplation.

"Robson," said the facilitator, "perhaps you'll start us off."

Robson opened the meeting with an unfortunate case of his mistaken identity, in which, having taken a menial role in a sportswear production and distribution company - on a paltry and (said Robson) somewhat exploitative contract - he determined to take his medicine in equanimous fashion; his colleagues and immediate supervisors, mistaking his serenity for something closer to a generally unrealistic sense of security - entirely out of context in the circumstances - developed a theory that this was a 'secret boss' project for television (even though there were no television cameras that they were aware of) and that he was, in fact, the head of the company. Eschewing any form of research that may have relieved them of their erroneous ideas, they set about a deferential programme to make him extremely happy and comfortable - assigning him the least odious tasks, impressing him with their own strenuous efforts in their own roles, generously donating ever more luxurious food items from their snap tins and so on, in the hope of favourable treatment later. Robson readily and regretfully admitted to the meeting that he soon gathered there had been some sort of mistake but had decided to enjoy the perks while he could, and was only found out when the real head of the company arrived unannounced one morning to lay everyone off.

As agreed with Northcott-Cornish, Creed was there to make one last attempt to get on with his driver re-training and had Nash along for company. Creed turned to his neighbour and whispered, "I still don't understand what this has got to do with road traffic offences."

"It's more of a multidisciplinary meeting really," said Nash.

This was the busiest meeting so far, in Creed's experience - twelve or thirteen participants gathered around the two rows of the circle. He realised this was going to take quite some time, and wished he had worked harder at the first meeting when it was just himself and Porter; perhaps he would have finished by now. But here he was, and he would have to sit through a dozen stories of mistakes, mischances and misconceptions today, most of which made little sense or had no relevance to Creed. It was more of a storytelling class, he thought.

While he had been distracted by his own misfortune, another participant sitting behind him had been invited to share the error of his ways and had started up with a new story. Creed had missed the name of this new respondent and he had missed the first half of his story, though it wasn't difficult to pick up the thread.

"...with the stress of it all, I had quite forgotten that all feedback should be seen as constructive and used appropriately. Instead I got into a terrible fury, found out when and where the next meeting would be, checked that he would be in attendance, and went along. Of course they tried to keep me out, but I was entirely furious, broke into the meeting, and confronted him. I deeply regret this, especially - "

Creed craned back over his shoulder. "Whealcoates!"

"Creed. I sincerely apologise for calling you a - "

"They're making you sit in the circle now?" wondered Creed.

"Shall we save the discussion for the next part of the session," suggested the facilitator, "and proceed with a momentary pause for thought, as is proper?"

Polite silence ensued.

After ten or eleven more stories, during a break for tea and a biscuit, Creed gathered Nash and Whealcoates to him for a conspiratorial discussion about the Corrective Measures Forum, Colloquium and all that Eustace Cove had told him.

"Preposterous!" said Whealcoates. He did seem genuinely apologetic for the insult and keen to make amends with any information he could provide.

"When will I be finished on this course?" demanded Creed, sensing an opportunity. But neither Whealcoates nor Nash could be sure of that, despite their eagerness to assist. With no end in sight Creed determined to take up Eustace Cove's suggestion, and visit the head office of the peculiar corporation that was running things around here. He whittled the address out of Whealcoates and was surprised to find it was within reach if he set out immediately. They tried to discourage him from anything rash.

"What about the programme," said Nash, "if you go now it will only set you back."

Creed was not to be put off, and left before the long talking session about Robson's identity crisis and Whealcoates' insult and all the rest of it started, where the errors of their ways would be reviewed and analysed, and strategic amends made.

"I hope it doesn't come as too much of a shock," said Whealcoates, as Creed slipped out of the meeting room.

Colloquium House

"Anita? What are you doing here?" A large digital counter on the wall ticked over from 4999 to 5000, and a bell chimed. Underneath the number, there was an explanation. It read, 'PEOPLE HELPED TODAY'. The bell chimed again and Creed was knocked to the floor by a diving security guard.

Getting into the headquarters of the Colloquium Corporation had gone as well as Eustace Cove predicted.

"I've got an appointment with Swales," Creed had said. There was nobody called Swales there, of course. The guard on reception went to the back office for clarification. Creed stormed the lift, the door closing out the cursing security guard. Following Eustace' advice, Creed went directly to the fifth floor. As he stepped out into the lobby, he could hear the guard stomping up the stairs, muttering into a radio, breathing heavily. Creed pushed through the plain doors marked 'Colloquium'.

"You must have an appointment to come in here. This isn't a public office." A smartly-dressed woman approached from behind another reception desk, radio in one hand and the other held up to stop him.

"I'm here to see Swales," said Creed, pushing past her and into the main room beyond. She followed him, making a fuss about untimely disruption, and he quickened his pace to keep a distance between them.

"Hello, this is Customer Onboarding, you're talking to Dev," said Dev, at a nearby desk, speaking through a headset to somebody on the line, "how can I navigate you to a desirable outcome today?"

In the long room, there must have been a hundred such stations. The receptionist blustered along behind as he caught fragments of one-sided telephone conversations. "You are through to Technical Services, what seems to be the problem?"

"Hello there, I'm pleased to advise you have won three hundred reward points today on your company loyalty card, I just need to take some details from you,"

"Shall we take a look at your account, madam, I am sure we can sort this out,"

"I'm afraid we don't handle life or death situations sir, but if you'll just hold on, I will connect you to The Samaritans." Creed stopped. It was Anita, from The Aureleian Society. And just alongside her was her colleague, Will. They were both wearing headsets.

"Anita," said Creed, "What are you doing here?" A bell chimed and Creed was tackled by security.

"Durgan," said Anita, "and Skipp."

Creed was on the floor, his cheek pressed into the abrasive carpet, the guard holding him in a wholly secure and somewhat uncomfortable position.

"W- what?" he managed to spit out.

Anita leaned down to him. "In here you call us Durgan, and Skipp. Company policy."

"Oh" said Creed, through a compressed face, "sorry."

They left him alone in a locked room with one chair, no windows and a broken photocopier. Northcott-Cornish came in briefly, looking disappointed. She told him she would bring him a cup of tea and a biscuit, but he didn't see her again. There was no sign of Durgan and Skipp. He banged once and called out but no-one came to see what the trouble was. They did not confiscate his phone, and he still had the card with the phone number on it. Not the Aureleian Society card, though he still had this too. But with Anita right outside, he didn't imagine calling the Society would do much good. He had another card.

"Eustace? It's Creed here. I seem to have got myself into a spot of bother."

The Outwith Group

"We're going to bring them down!" growled Eustace Cove, clapping a fist into his open hand. Ivan, Robin, Helen,

Gram, Brian, the twins, Fenton, Martin, Miranda, Caroline, Vincenzo, and the rest of the Outwith Group raised a cheer in support of their leader. Creed felt obliged to join in, of course; it was only polite. They had been very welcoming.

The escape from Colloquium HQ could not have been any smoother.

Creed had barely put his telephone away when he heard the door of his photocopier cell unlock. He waited for someone to come in, but the door never opened. He listened at the door - everything sounded perfectly regular in the busy office outside. He tried the door handle, opened the door, stepped out. There did not appear to be anyone waiting for him, and all of the call centre operatives seemed to be fully engaged in their work, apart from Will Skipp, his Aureleian doorstep visitor, who was not at his desk.

"Mr. Swales?" A woman he would come to know as 'Miranda' approached him with a knowing wink; "this way please." They walked the length of the office, unnoticed, until they reached the far end. The digital counter clicked over from 5999 to 6000. Miranda unlocked a door marked 'Store' which opened into a large empty room where a man he would come to know as 'Vincenzo' was waiting.

"Come with me," said Vincenzo, opening a door on the opposite side of the room. It led to a staircase, down and out into a narrow street alongside Colloquium House. An unremarkable car was waiting, with Eustace Cove in the front passenger seat. Miranda got in the driver seat, Creed and Vincenzo in the back.

"Welcome to The Outwith Group," said a man Creed would come to know as 'Ivan', back at an unremarkable industrial unit across town, "tea and biscuits? We don't stint on the Garibaldis here, you know."

It was strictly first name terms at the Outwith Group. And plenty of biscuits.

They discussed various unrealistic-sounding plans for bringing down the corporation, but Creed found it difficult to get a word in or find out precisely when his retraining would be complete and he could get his driving licence cleared, free of endorsement.

"They'll always find an excuse," said Fenton, "and that's why we have to bring them down."

"You mean I won't ever get to the end of my programme?" wondered Creed.

"Brian here has an open ticket with The Self-Help Desk that has been unresolved for thirteen years," explained Eustace, unhelpfully, "and Fenton - Fenton, when did The Aureleians first knock on your door?"

"1984," said Fenton.

"1984!" exclaimed Eustace, "We don't want your help any more, Colloquium!"

"We don't want your help any more, Colloquium!" chanted the group.

"The Outwith Group helps those who help themselves!" intoned Eustace.

"The Outwith Group helps those who help themselves!" they replied.

"No more help! Out with Colloquium!" he said.

"Out! Out! Out!" they agreed, waving their fists enthusiastically at each other.

"Is there any chance someone could drive me home," asked Creed, "I mean, before you stop helping?"

Nash

There was a knock at the door.

"Anita! I mean, Durgan!" said Creed, "and Nash! What are you two doing here?"

His rescuers Miranda and Eustace from the Outwith Group had not long dropped Creed home in their remarkably anonymous car, and promised that together, united, they would bring down the corporation and all their helpful meddling intent. He was just making himself a cup of tea when The Aureleians called.

"We're making a visit on behalf of The Aureleian Society," said Anita, at the doorstep, "and you can call me Anita, when I'm an Aureleian."

"And I'm Arthur," said Nash, "You have heard of the Aureleians, and you're familiar with our work of course?"

"You'd better come in," said Creed. He wanted to tell them about The Outwith Group.

Arthur Nash and Anita explained that they were there to listen, to attach no value judgments, and to help strategise for a new way of moving forward that would make him happy and ensure that he could continue to make good with the world. He was still, after all - said Nash - a decent person with a positive contribution to make. Creed provided the tea and, remembering Ivan, a whole plate of biscuits.

"It's terribly unfortunate that you've got wrapped up with this Cove and his 'Outwits' as we like to call them," said Nash, "no doubt they have muddied the water considerably. We're here to help clear things up."

They discussed Creed's raid on Colloquium House.

"I wanted to find out what it was all about, yes," admitted Creed, "but now I'm wondering if the whole thing has been a waste of time and perhaps I should've just… well, I really don't know. Finished the programme? Is that even possible?"

Arthur wanted to reassure him that it was more than possible, that he was on the path to a full clean licence, his fine would be revoked, and that if he could just be patient with the programme, he would undoubtedly reap rewards that even he, Nash, could not predict in the moment.

"I don't want to come across excessively hyperbolic, but it might change the course of your life," he speculated. That was rather familiar, thought Creed.

"Will you come to our annual conference?" asked Nash, "I think you will find all the answers you need there."

"Alright" said Creed.

Universal Undo

"Dammit man, it's Cove! Eustace Cove! Of all the… Cove is here. He's wearing a moustache, but it's him alright. What the devil?"

Months had passed since Creed's initial transgression that brought him into contact with these peculiar people and their infuriating obsession with fixing things in the proper manner. They still hadn't fixed things for him, really. Nash had at least rescued him from the little joker on the front desk, but things had quickly turned sour at the Annual Universal Undo Conference.

Nash frowned more. "I don't see him. Are you sure? It can't be."

"What is he up to? Coming here? This is no good, Nash. This is no good at all!"

Creed headed for the small group of people making pre-conference small-talk on the far side of the auditorium. One man broke off and strode toward a side exit. "Oh no you don't, Cove!" muttered Creed, changing direction.

Cove slipped through the side exit, closing the door behind him. When Creed went through, he found a curved corridor to left and right, with no sign of Cove. Nash came through the door after him.

"Look, Creed - " he started.

"He's up to something, Nash," said Creed, "he's going to bring the organisation down, he said it himself. Where the devil is he? You go that way, and I'll go this…"

Northcott-Cornish appeared around the corner.

"Northcott-Cornish!" exclaimed Creed, "We have a situation - Eustace Cove is here!"

"I'm not sure - " started Nash again.

"Skipp!" said Creed, clicking his fingers, "Skipp knows!"

"What's this now?" - Northcott-Cornish.

Creed strode back into the auditorium, toward the group who had been making small-talk - allegedly - with Eustace Cove. One of them was Will, the Aureleian who had been to his house - Skipp, as he was known at Colloquium House where he worked in the call centre on the fifth floor. Northcott-Cornish and Nash followed along behind.

"Now look, Creed - " said Northcott-Cornish. But Creed was already ahead of her and approaching the small-talkers.

"Skipp!" called Creed, "Skipp - you're with the Outwith Group!"

"Creed, I - " started Skipp.

"Don't pretend now, Skipp, come clean. I know Eustace is here - I saw you talking to him. When they rescued me from Colloquium House… you weren't at your desk. You let Miranda in, didn't you? You unlocked the door to the room I was trapped in. You're their inside man!"

"Creed, I - " started Skipp again.

"Really Creed," said Northcott-Cornish, assertively, "why don't you come with me, we can talk this through in a more private setting."

Northcott-Cornish found a small office close to reception to discuss matters with Creed. She sent Nash to get Eustace Cove, who had been on his way to the bathroom when Creed spotted him. She ordered some tea and a biscuit.

"We probably have some explaining to do" she said.

DVLA

"I just want to know how much longer I have got on my driver re-training course?" asked Creed. Even after the Annual Universal Undo Conference and the grand reveal, his associates at Colloquium still hadn't been able to confirm how many more sessions he would have to attend. So he called the Driver & Vehicles Licensing Agency.

"Only one session, Mr. Creed," said the agent on the phone.

"One more session to go?"

"No sir, you just have to attend one session overall. Our records indicate you did that some time ago."

"My licence is clean?"

"Perfectly clean, Mr. Creed."

Explainer

"What do you mean, 'he's one of us'?" asked Creed, "he's the leader of the Outwith Group!"

Skipp, Nash and Eustace Cove joined them in the small office of the Imperial Hotel, where Northcott-Cornish was about to engage in a convoluted description of Experiential Scaffold Modelling, by way of explaining the confusion.

"We probably have some explaining to do" she said.

Northcott-Cornish explained.

"I see," said Creed. "Well I have to admit none of those stories in Corrective Measures meetings rang true."

"Clearly we will have to work on those," acknowledged Northcott-Cornish.

"But what about Miranda and Vincenzo and the rest of the Outwith Group - they seemed so... passionate?"

They were true believers of the Outwith mantras - said Eustace Cove - and were on a separate programme with its own narrative arc; one with a different set of objectives that was more open ended. One with first names and more biscuits - said Eustace. "We thought you might enjoy the counter culture of the Outwith approach but clearly, although you were polite enough to go along with the chanting, it wasn't for you."

"You mean to say," said Creed, "poor Fenton... since 1984? And Brian's open ticket on the Self-Help Desk? You've kept them on the programme that long?"

Fenton's whole life was built around his weekly visits from The Aureleians - said Eustace - and routine was extremely important to him; while Brian hadn't called the Self-Help

Desk in over a decade, where, if he had only checked, he would've found he had been closed years ago. "They just enjoy the weekly planning sessions to bring down the corporation, a little bit of chanting, and the occasional dramatic rescue from HQ facilitated by our man on the inside."

"Skipp," said Creed.

"Anyone," clarified Northcott-Cornish.

"Nevertheless," continued Creed, "I have a hard time imagining why… all this… surely it would have been more efficient all round to simply enforce a fixed penalty and an endorsement on my licence?"

"But not as much fun," said Nash.

Epilogue

FOURTH MEETING

"Are we ready?" asked Whealcoates, at no-one in particular.

"Then we begin," said the host.

There was a long pause. A very long pause.

"Would you care to open the meeting, Smith?" said Whealcoates.

The new woman sitting at about a quarter to ten in the circle of chairs explained how she had been caught by the speed check camera on the One Way System, and expressed a desire to avoid a fine, if she possibly could.

"Thank you Smith, a very interesting first contribution. I'm sure there is plenty to think about there. Shall we take a moment?" Whealcoates introduced another of his uncomfortably long silences.

"Creed? Would you care to follow on?" asked the host eventually, of the man sitting at half past five in the seating arrangement.

What Happened At The Ossington

Prologue
The Ossington Coffee Palace

Standing on the corner of North Gate and Beastmarket Hill in Newark there surely could have been no finer dole office in all of England. Built by a Victorian aristocrat to counter the degeneracy of the demon drink amongst the poor people of the town and to give working men a more salubrious space for the pursuit of healthy leisures in their time off, when their tiny hovel houses so full of children and women and noise and cooking and laundry afforded no rest for the wicked, it was a striking visual statement at the gateway to the town. A bequest to the people of Newark that they might become more erudite and more at ease, and less drunk, this house of temperance was amply furnished with coffee rooms, billiard rooms, reading rooms, rest rooms, bedrooms and an American bowling alley. Becoming a job centre in later life seems perhaps a natural maturing, or diminishing, of intent to help the poor to help themselves.

So desirable and spacious were the accommodations that the government twice requisitioned it during war time, and twice tried to avoid giving it back. After the first World War it took several years for the trustees of the late Viscountess Ossington, Lady Charlotte Denison, to reacquire the building from the Army who resisted vigorously. Lady Ossington had built the magnificent mock-Tudor coffee palace at her own expense, a whopping £25,000, and made provisions for it to remain in the hands of the people of the town - and to remain free of liquor. After the second World War, the Ministry of Health were even more vigorous in their desire to retain the palatial facility they had used as a wartime telephony centre, and this time succeeded in wresting the building from the trustees. It became a job centre and then a tax office, and later, when they had better options - likely cheaper to maintain - it was sold on to become at various times a fish and chip shop, a cheap hotel, a fun pub and a pizza restaurant. Today, as of writing, it is vacant - not for the first time - though the upper floors are divided now into exclusive and desirable private apartments.

The building has never been a commercial success. This would have been of no surprise to the Viscountess Ossington, who in her original provision stated:

A large building, like our tavern and hostelry, cannot be kept without considerable expense, and it is idle to suppose it will be a paying concern in the pecuniary sense of the word.

When the government - having forced the Ossington out of the hands of the trustees and out of the possession of the town of Newark - had no further use for the building they sold it on to private concerns in the 1980s rather than handing it back to the town. A chequered period of failed commercial ventures, insolvencies, planning disputes, travesties of liquor-fuelled ill-behaviour and intermittent periods of extended unoccupied vacancy have ensued. Lady Charlotte could have told them it wouldn't work - indeed, she fairly did tell them.

Galloway's Temperance
A Conversation at The Bean & Vine

"Here he is," someone said appreciatively, coming through the shop door.

I was in a Newark café, taking my morning coffee and contemplating the architecture of the square. In particular I was once again considering the conservation of the original sign over the shopfront at 5, Market Place: since moving to the town four years ago, I'd come to very much appreciate the words Pharmaceutical Chemist, gold painted serif carved into a dark wood panel. I liked the font, reminiscent somehow of Stephenson, Blake & Company's *Algerian* typeface though less loathsome - more authentic perhaps - than the inappropriately overused modern Linotype version popularised by Microsoft; and how the current residents of the shop, unrelated to pharmaceuticals - although arguably, perhaps not - had preserved the signage and mounted their own, The Bean & Vine, clearly above it. I thought it indicative of a respect for, perhaps pride in, the typographical heritage of this place. (The Bean & Vine type itself is also nicely rendered in a decorative yet sensitive capitalised serif font, with a modest flourish to the ampersand, apparently cut from a dark steel or tin plate and welded with fair craft into a decorative supporting frame of black-painted rods curved and mounted by bracket to the Georgian building.)

Nursing a full-bodied caffè americano[1] I was surprised by the appearance of an old acquaintance of many years, the

---

[1] Sourced from Nottingham roasters 200° Coffee: their signature espresso blend "Brazilian Love Affair", which the company describe as 'a balanced espresso with a broad appeal, roasted medium dark for a full-bodied flavour with notes of dark chocolate that is bold enough to stand up in milky drinks'. Not that I take milk with my coffee.

inveterate storyteller and champion liar Galloway, come in to the Bean & Vine to see me. Surprised because, in my experience, he rarely ventured far these days from his stool at the bar of The Local Tap, some miles out of town. He ordered a double espresso and joined me for what turned out to be one of his contemplations on the art of digression.

"How's the writing going," he asked me, "keeping up appearances, I hope?"

"I've not known you to take coffee in the middle of the day," I said, ignoring the quip.

He explained that he was observing a period of temperance for the good of his health, though I rather suspected it was no coincidence him being here now and declaring restraint from the modest delights of the ale, given that I had recently told him I was working on a story about the town's spectacular Victorian coffee house, the Ossington. Of his many delights in passing on false wisdom to the unwary, the opportunity to muddy the waters of historical research was irresistible.

History may be written by the victors, he had once told me, but truth is a contagion spread by bold deceivers. At the time - some years ago - he was trying to convince me of the importance of persevering with his walking tours of old time Newark when the local Historical Society was battling to have him drummed out of town. A man dressed as a Victorian cutpurse had then just recently attempted to assault him while he decried the famous Newark printer Mr. Ridge - a cutpurse himself of sorts, who had villainously profiteered from the success of our local Lord Byron during his lifetime by selling under-the-counter pamphlets of the poet's early observations on the varying degrees of moral lassitude amongst the townswomen of Newark. Galloway was quite sure the contemporary mugger (disguised in vintage attire) was a man of Historical Society connections.

This was at a time when The Ossington Coffee Palace had recently closed as a national training centre for Mr. Haddock[2], the since liquidated chip shop chain. In between a lurid account of the trials and tribulations of riding the cuckstool under the walls of Newark Castle and the legend of Prince Rupert's lion-eating dog Fydoe, on his walking tours Galloway would tell bemused tourists that when the environment agency discovered Mr. Haddock himself was nothing but a bleached and reconstituted brown trout scooped out of the sticky shallows of the Trent, the writing was on the wall for the piscine enterprise which went into financial meltdown soon afterward. The Historical Society had occasionally sent a stooge to dispute Galloway's accounts, but soon took to a persistent letter-writing campaign to the Newark Advertiser from a safe distance instead, when the storyteller began to get violently defensive of his position.

---

[2] When I started my research into the Coffee Palace I was reminded of my one direct experience of the restaurant chain. My former wife, a native of Birkenhead in The Wirral, had introduced me to many local delights of a north west high street during a home-coming visit in our early days together including Stolen From Ivor, pre-nationwide Gregg's Bakery, Sharples News and Mr. Haddock. I recall we had a near silent but vicious disagreement in the chip shop after I had taken offence to someone dribbling their half-masticated chips onto their plate at the next table. It was only a month after my mother had died of pneumonia, at the end of a long battle with Alzheimer's Disease, and I was sensitive to manifestations of the struggles she faced in her terminal decline. Today I have no problem with dribbling or most other symptoms of late-stage dementia, though people rummaging endlessly through handbags whilst hoping for a reminder of what they are actually looking for remains a potent trigger. My wife quickly forgave my temporary intolerance but I don't think we ever went back to Mr. Haddock and eventually we were divorced.

'This is just the way I walk!' would become his trademark retort to any disruptive element on his tours, a precursor to lashing out with his fist.

"So," said Galloway, bringing me back to the present, there in the Bean & Vine, "you are planning, I assume, to write about what happened at The Ossington?"

This was an obvious cue, and I briefly considered how I might skirt around it, preventing my companion from launching into whatever dubious lecture he had prepared for me. I drew a blank.

"Well," I said, "I suppose that depends on what you mean by 'what happened at The Ossington'. I've got to write something, anyway."

"I've a few things in mind," I added, as an afterthought. Of course, he easily ignored this limp defence and proceeded to assist in my research with his - probably - unique grasp of local folklore.

Fugitive Piece
Provisioning at Porter's

Lunchtime was giving way to mid-afternoon when Galloway finished his third short coffee and his long story about a message in a bottle. The staff were eager to clear the tables now, encouraging us to move on. Early-closing Wednesday afternoon, a determination of the Shop Hours Act of 1904 that was repealed everywhere else in 1994, is to this day voluntarily maintained by Newark cafés along with early-closing Mondays, early-closing Tuesdays, Thursdays, Fridays, most Saturdays and definitely Sundays which are late-opening and very-early-closing-indeed. It was time to move.

Even on market days one could at least see the shop sign above Porter's Provisions on the far side of the square from the window seats of The Bean & Vine and on quieter days the red-and-white painted butcher's shop looked a neat compliment to the stripes of the market stall canopies. I was reminded, while Galloway delivered his wild theory on the truth behind what happened at The Ossington, that I needed a resupply of orange tea. It makes a light change from all the heavy coffees I am inclined to consume. After saying my goodbyes to my volunteer research assistant, the brazen meddler, I headed across the square to join the queue at Porter's coffee counter - it's a small shop and there was clearly a bit of a rush on.

"Shouldn't you be at home writing?" someone said behind me. When I turned around there was my friend Linda from The Writers Group.

"Shouldn't you?" I joked, by way of greeting.

"I'm half way between the Green Dragon and the White Horse," she said. I wasn't sure at all if that was code for something.

"Research," she added by way of clarification. Ah yes, the drinking story.

"How many pubs are you writing about?" I asked. While we waited for provisions, we fell to discussing our stories and our progress and the challenges of researching the historic buildings of Newark. I told her that since the building I was writing about was closed to the public, I was having to drink coffee all over town in the name of my studies whilst I contemplated how to accurately represent what happened at The Ossington. Fortunately, as Linda explained to me, having a range of public houses to write about and most of them still in business, she was finding the research perfectly accessible. As I was ordering my orange redbush at the counter, Linda mentioned that it must be a popular day for research as she had not long passed our colleague Sam coming out of the Travelodge hotel and Nick, who was one of the Chief Writers of The Writers Group, on his way to Thorpe's Warehouse to measure how far you would have to fall from the upper floor to the lock below.

"…and here now," she nodded, "is Abigail. Are you researching too?"

Abigail, a prolific member of the Writers Group, was just coming out of Porter's butcher shop next door to the coffee counter with a parcel of fine cuts and a stewing bone. She told us that, as it happened, she was also on the research trail; we took a moment to discuss our stories and our progress and the challenges of researching the historic buildings of Newark. The butcher shop, of course, used to be the premises of Mr. Ridge the Printer, and Abigail was planning to write a story about Fanny.

"Fanny?" I asked.

"Fanny and Bryon," Abigail explained.

"Bryon?" asked Linda.

"Byron," said Abigail, "did I say Bryon?"

"Ah, Byron," said Linda, "maybe I misheard, I thought you said Bryon."

I thought she said Bryon too.

Abigail went on to outline the premise of her story, and we all agreed it sounded quite perfect for The Writers Group next anthology. I briefly wondered how I was going to make my story as interesting as all these brilliant ideas that were floating about, each of which seemed to be better formed and more interesting than my own. Perhaps I needed to spend more time with Galloway, who never doubted himself or his stories.

Linda looked rather distant all of a sudden, and then said, "There's Clair."[3]

We all waved to Clair.

"Well," said Linda, "I better get on. I've got a lot of ground to cover today."

We three agreed that if we were to meet the deadline for this writing project, we should probably all get on, and arranged to meet later for a sharing at the LetsXcape Together Café. I glanced up at Clair and she was still waving. I wondered if she was planning on coming to the meeting too.

---

[3] It took a while for Abigail and I to locate Clair, who was one of the Chief Writers of The Writers Group.

"Where?" I said. *Abigail cupped a hand over her eyes, scanning in the direction Linda was looking.*

"Up there," *said Linda, pointing - and there she was, on top of the church tower, at the base of the spire, a long way up indeed.*

"What…?" *I wondered.*

"She's researching St. Mary Magdalene's for her story, I suppose," *said Abigail.*

"Up there?" *I asked.*

Clair began to wave.

"Is she waving?" *said Linda.*

"I think so," *said Abigail.*

"Waving, or panicking?" *I wondered. She was definitely waving with both arms anyway.*

"She told me she doesn't have a head for heights," *Linda pointed out.*

"Waving, I think," *said Abigail, reassuringly,* "yes, definitely waving not panicking."

I wasn't so sure. Waving not holding on, I thought.

"It looks like we're all going the extra mile today," *said Linda.*

Message In A Bottle
Under The Foundations of The Ossington

When I first undertook to write about the Ossington Coffee Palace, perhaps two things immediately leapt out at me that, in the end, were not the things I have written about here. One, most obviously, was the ghost story. Before I knew anything, before I had read a single line of research, I knew to expect the inevitable equation:

historic building + (fiction researcher / coffee) = haunted house

'You know there is a ghost in the cellars there, don't you?'

How do you tell a generous interviewee you don't believe all that mumbo-jumbo without offending them? I will come to that later, on page 85, precisely three sections from now.

The second teaser that elicited more enthusiasm on my part was the message in a bottle buried by one of the architects of the building. Placed under the foundation stone laid at the commencement of construction of The Ossington, the bottle was reported to have contained a set of freshly minted coins of the realm and a hand-written copy of the speech by the temperance philanthropist Lady Charlotte Denison, commissioner and funder of the Coffee Palace, delivered from the first floor balcony upon the opening of the tavern on 23 November 1882.

Why, in the end, did I reject this potentially rich vein of story when finalising my plans for this essay? My source tells me the message in a bottle no longer exists, and neither does the cash.

"A scurrilous ragamuffin dug up the bottle three weeks later," Galloway had told me, "and spent the proceeds in The Ram."

What about the hand-written speech, I wondered.

"He couldn't read," said Galloway.

The Way I Walk
A Guided Tour of Old-Time Newark

1. INGLEDEW MILL, MILL GATE:
A mechanic of the name Beck was making repairs to Ingledew's windmill, which had been badly neglected for some years - Ingledew being a legendary skinflint and all - and was fixing one of the sails when the faulty brake failed. It being a particularly windy spring day, the sails started up at a fair pace and John Beck was caught by the ankle. Alerted by his yelling, a miller on the premises managed eventually to engage the brake, by which time Beck had performed more than a hundred revolutions of the windmill and complained of headaches and dizziness for the rest of his sorry life.

2. SPECSAVERS, MIDDLE GATE:
On this site once stood Newark's first theatre, operated by the famous Robertson Family who had a monopoly of 'the Lincoln Circuit' of theatres in the region. The Newark branch was not a great success, blighted by a lack of interest in the town, and was eventually lost in the development of the Buttermarket. By coincidence it was in Newark Theatre that the seeds of the demise of the most famous Lincoln - that would be Abraham - were planted, so to speak. Miss Booth of Covent Garden was booked for the theatrical season of 1828 and a few months later she and her husband Junius Brutus emigrated to the United States with their new-born son, John Wilkes Booth, conceived after a performance of The Busy Body in Newark. J. Wilkes Booth grew up and maintained an interest in the family business, creating a major drama when he shot and killed President Lincoln at Ford's Theatre in Washington, DC.

3. QUEENS COURT, off KIRK GATE:

The industrialisation of Newark was no small thing, though small things were often made of it. The watch and clockmaker John Priest made the world's smallest steam engine that weighed half an ounce and was housed inside a walnut shell. The flywheel was three quarters of an inch in diameter and the engine could be kept in motion for several minutes at a time.

4. GOVERNOR'S HOUSE, MARKET SQUARE:

In between being the most important house for the most important person in the town and a Gregg's Bakery, the Governor's House was also The Home of Football, though it gets little credit for being the place where the global sport was invented. This may be because even back then it was still operating as a bakery, producing a large portion of the flour and water footballs that were used for the first ever matches which took place in the Square. Every Hercules Clay Day (March 10th) the bakery helped produce the 3,654 loaves required for extended games between the town's Rowdies and Rogues, and the practice dates back at least fifty years prior to the start of The Football League.

5. No. 5, MOUNT LANE:

At six o'clock one stormy Sunday evening of August 1831 there was a terrible flash that permanently blinded the minister in the pulpit of St. Mary's, accompanied at the instant by a tremendous peal of thunder which shook the church and houses all around. The electric fluid was seen to descend with great velocity and strike the steeple of the church, tearing some of the ornaments off as it descended to the east. It then darted across the churchyard into Mount Lane and entered a house through a door which was open, striking a redolent and ungodly person named Cox (who should've been in church) on the foot, but the force of it being spent, did no damage as it immediately vanished into smoke, leaving a smell of sulphur behind for which Cox sincerely apologised.

6. THE WHEATSHEAF, SLAUGHTERHOUSE LANE:

They always loved their shoes in Newark, once showing their prodigious artistry for the craft by making the largest leather boot in the world at four feet high and six feet long (it was only an ankle boot) which in today's sizes would probably fit a size one hundred and eleven foot. Impressive though it was, there was no buyer for it and records show the left boot was never made. In old-time Newark there was also something of a festival spirit to October, shoe-related, when the Disciples of Crispin came to town for their annual party at The Wheatsheaf, dedicated as they were to the worship of the patron saint of shoemaking.

7. AIR & SPACE INSTITUTE, FRIARY LANE:

Newark has always been at the heart of the space race, ever since Mr. Green the Aeronaut inflated his first balloon at the old gas works nearby and became the first man to fly over the town. The concept of the parachute was also first proposed in Newark when one of Mr. Green the Aeronaut's passengers fell out of his basket at a thousand feet and lived to tell the tale despite severe injury. Mrs. Graham was sustained by a sturdy parasol and several layers of expansive skirts before landing in gardens close to the town centre.

8. ALMS HOUSES, LINCOLN ROAD:

In the listings of proceedings of the town magistrates and the district session courts, inanimate objects and animals deemed responsible for the serious injury or death of a person might be subject to the order of *deo dandum*, that is to say, 'given to God'. For example, a young man died after being run over by his own cart, and since his own incompetence could not be proved in the case, it was declared an accidental death, with a *deodand* placed upon the specific wheel that crushed his head. Similarly a cat tried for attempted murder of an old widow at the Alms Houses was 'given to God', though whether the outcome was especially pleasing to the cat is not reported.

Downing Tools
A Conversation at The Ram

Speaking of liars:

    I took a break from my research to hold a remote-from-work meeting, which is a thing now. Over a much-needed and rather indulgent afternoon cortado[4] at The Ram[5][6], my colleague Tyger Bourne[7] and I were analysing a recent encounter with a bare-faced liar we had not enjoyed so much in the course of a recent working day. Outside of researching historical buildings of the temperance movement, wholly unpaid and therefore more in the realm of 'hobby', as Galloway might dismissively describe my literary pursuits, it is necessary for me to earn an income elsewhere and I am largely occupied by the interminable bureaucracy of the modern secondary education system. Ms. Bourne and I as co-directors of such an establishment had recently not enjoyed an encounter with Mr. Phillips the woodwork teacher. Encounters with Mr. Phillips invariably fall into one of two categories - tedious or exasperating (and sometimes both). As a general rule of thumb all avoidable encounters with Mr. Phillips are rigorously avoided, actual encounters being only the entirely unavoidable. One such encounter was a walk-and-talk in the school gardens, subsequent to a complaint from Miss Gayle, the horticultural teacher.

---

[4] *A Spanish equivalent to the Italian macchiato or French noisette, in which steamed milk is applied to reduce the acidity of the coffee - a welcome smoothing off of the roast after several unadulterated drinks earlier in the day.*

[5] *On Castle Gate, directly opposite the castle itself, The Ram Hotel was frequently cited in contemporaneous local newspaper articles upon commission of The Coffee Palace by Viscountess Ossington as illustrative of the relative iniquities of drink in the town of Newark at the time, a*

She had a point. A beloved giant needle palm in the school grounds had been the victim of an inelegant, nay brutal, emasculation - the metre-long leaves of the great bush each severed square across at their widest girth, just beneath where they would taper to a fine, sharp zenith, shortened by half and blunted to impotent flat-ended amputees, poor imitations of their former glory as an array of eye-catching spikes. It was a pointless vandalism: Miss Gayle had cried with the nihilism of it all when she delivered her complaint. (She was also the philosophy cover teacher on standby for the perpetually troubled and often indisposed Mrs. Nallis.)

The evidence against Mr. Phillips was overwhelming, if not conclusive: (i) he often took his most disruptive groups out of the workshop to 'burn off energy' in more useful repair and maintenance activities around the school grounds; (ii) in his brief period as general caretaker he instituted a slash-and-burn policy toward the wilder sections of the gardens for health and safety reasons, proposing to cut down trees to improve line-of-sight in behaviour management, increasing the application of concrete to as great a surface area as he could reasonably get away with and killing as many insects as possible to prevent bites, stings and flailing panic attacks in lessons; (iii) he didn't like Miss Gayle whom he was fond of dismissing by quoting in two-fingered quotation mark signs and was resentful of for losing garden management to (for reasons see (ii) previous;

---

dangerous and rotten tavern at the heart of the ruination of the Victorian working class family. Today you could hardly imagine it - a comfortable and civilised pub-restaurant, the author particularly recommends a light afternoon meal of pole-and-line caught tuna steak with coconut rice and of course their smooth, dark blend Italian coffees (wine is an option of course but it was, after all, a business lunch). Tyger Bourne opted for the risotto con funghi, equally delightful.

[6] *Public houses do not follow early-closing afternoons, even in Newark.*

(iv) he often complained, as a self-proclaimed health and safety expert, that the needle palm was dangerous for over-excited pupils engaged in climbing, leaping and play fighting; and (v) in the lesson before the discovery of egregious pruning he had been seen taking his naughty boys of class 11 to the tool shed before unleashing them in the gardens.

For want of actual video footage the charge could not be upheld without his voluntary admission and on our walk-and-talk with Mr. Phillips, he flatly denied it, felt it unnecessary to speculate on alternative explanations, and - unusually for him, an expansive provider of the minutiae of his fascinating life and thus, a crashing bore - maintained a stoic one-line defence from which he would neither deviate nor expand.

"Well, it wasn't us," he said, "we didn't go near it." He used this line repeatedly to cover the whole of the garden, the tool shed in particular, and the offended needle palm itself. He repeated it until we shook our heads in exasperation and went back to our office to discuss it further without him[8], and then on to The Ram a few days later for more biting reflection over coffee and lunch.

Negotiating the increasingly difficult tightrope of balancing staff satisfaction, productivity and employment law, Tyger Bourne often wished that it was still acceptable to yell at staff to encourage better results and issue disciplinary edicts

---

[7] Yes, really. Whether she was christened with it, or whether she chose it to match her fiery mien and combustible personality, I could not say. There was no point asking Tyger Bourne herself, she was another of those unreliable narrators I had a habit of picking up as friends or associates.

[8] Mr. Phillips excused himself the next day, staying home with a vaguely described and minor-sounding ailment which took eleven months to sufficiently clear in order that he might resume his teaching duties. This put his absence record even below that of Mrs. Nallis and her recurring existential crises. Some staff referred to him as 'a ghost', an epithet we usually reserved for perpetually-absent children.

without conclusive evidence. Common sense, she called it. In the case of Mr. Phillips, I was inclined to agree. I wondered if, in trying to be delicate, we had allowed him to brush us off too easily. I wondered, as I often did, if we had been working in a more acceptably frank environment - like, say, a building site - whether we might have had a more constructive conversation in which forcefully-made observations on our part might lead to some accommodation of truth.

I recount this here because it does have a bearing on matters of The Ossington folk history:

"Oh, he absolutely wouldn't get away with it there," said Tyger Bourne, referring to our theoretical building site. She went on to describe an incident where a friend of a friend had known of a builder who stole a colleague's angle grinder.

"Absolute flat denial," she said, about the incident when the injured party asked for his grinder back, "bare faced and brazen lying."

Apparently, a round of violence settled the dispute.

"A few of them dragged him off the site," she said, "and dumped him on the road outside. He staggered off, blood all over his face, and never came back. Left all his own gear, refused to come and collect it. Never asked for his pay."

I couldn't see this working on Mr. Phillips without a full employment tribunal and a hefty fine, but Tyger Bourne reflected that summary justice was nonetheless an underrated feature of some nostalgic past she was rather fond of.

"I wonder what he told his friends and family," I said, "about being so roundly spanked."

"He probably lied, of course," said Tyger Bourne, "they always do."

Maybe he told them he saw a ghost, I thought. It was the only acceptable reason, as a burly testosterone-fuelled construction worker, to refuse to go back to pick up your tools. And maybe, I thought, that was a standard excuse of chastised builders everywhere, a guild secret passed from generation to generation. "I'm never going back there, it's bloody terrifying."

Gin On The Balcony
A Look Inside The Ossington

Rita the truck driver had invited me up to take a look around her apartment at The Ossington. She'd already told me about the hauntings and the cold corners and the 'strange goings-on in the middle of the night' earlier that summer at the Newark Book Festival. I wasn't much interested in the superstitious or the irrational but I didn't tell Rita that because I wanted to go upstairs. That is to say, to the assembly room (also referred to - without any historical accuracy that I could validate - as 'the old ballroom') to get a bit of a feel for the setting. I wanted to understand how what happened at The Ossington could have happened at all, and where, and if not why then certainly how and under what circumstances. I brought her a bottle of expensive-looking gin.

Though the recent history of The Ossington is a rather turbulent matter of one financial ruin after another, the fabric of the building at least has come out with some net gain since being released from government oversight: the shoddy office partitioning and false ceilings have given way to elegant restorations, particularly upstairs where dark oak panelled walls and the full glory of the sculpted cornices and plaster of Paris ceiling roses give Rita's spacious apartment an authentic Victorian luxury we agreed could not be found further south for anyone but the gilded millionaire. Despite the palatial space - I could see why you would call it an old ballroom - and the sensitively integrated open plan contemporary kitchen, the neat bathroom and elegant Country Homes feature bedroom (though surprisingly not with four-poster period bed) what drew most of my attention was the large canvas, three quarters worked in oils in a lush contemporary abstract style which I now recall as mostly lemons, browns and oranges with deft touches in the green spectrum, proud on its easel at the centre of the open room and surrounded by a clutter of jars and bottles, paints and brushes, palettes and palette knives.

I no more knew that Rita was a painter than I did she was a truck driver, before I came upstairs. The painting was astonishing. Rita was thoroughly modest about the whole thing and distracted me with a glass of gin from the bottle I had brought, spoke briefly about her career as an artist and using the apartment as the perfect inspiration for a new series of works, and then changed the subject abruptly as soon as she could.

"You know there is a ghost in the cellars here, don't you?"

We had moved to the balcony overlooking the gardens and the river, where Lady Charlotte herself bestowed the Ossington upon the deserving poor with her speech that they might be happier in their lives, and I turned the conversation back toward the quality of the light by remarking on the sunsets over Tolney Lane encampment, such a scenic setting for the painterly type. I knew a thing or two about that after all, living as I did on the riverside myself just up past the castle. We went inside for another gin, and I hoped not to have to discuss the ghosts of aristocrats past.

"The reason I got in touch with The Writers Group," explained Rita, "was because I want to write a book about what I've done for the last twenty years. People often remark, 'you should write a book', and now I'm here, in this place, I think I will. I just need a bit of help with formatting."

"A book about painting?" - I wondered.

"About my truck," she clarified. This was when I learned Rita was also a famous truck driver.

"You can look me up on the internet," she said, probably because I looked like I might not believe her[9]. She told me all about her extraordinary adventures, and her famous truck

---

[9] *I did believe her but nevertheless did look her up later that evening, and everything was entirely as she said it was.*

which was now parked in storage down in Carcassonne. We had another gin each and then she told me it was about time for her to be getting on, and therefore it was time for me to go. But she had arranged for an introduction to Jeb, she said, who was her neighbour, and who had an encyclopaedic knowledge of The Ossington.

We knocked on at Jeb's place next door, in what had apparently been 'the other half' of the ballroom. After a long delay, the door opened to an old fellow in a white vest, sliders and lounge pants. He already had two steaming mugs of coffee prepared, though Rita announced she needed to get on and would leave me to it. Jeb was clearly a famous rock and roller of a bygone age who probably toured with a young Dylan before anyone had even heard of him. His long white hair, generous jewellery and the American accent were patent giveaways. I immediately surmised he had retired on modest royalties to lead as close to English Manor House retirement as he could afford. I was quite certain he would have spent the last twenty years accumulating all the key details on what happened at The Ossington at a depth to which I could not hope to do justice.

"You know there is a ghost in the cellars here, right?"

As it happened, Jeb was unable to fill in as many details as I might have hoped but he did give me a guided tour of cold spots in his apartment while I nursed the instant coffee he had kindly furnished. That was boiling hot. He hadn't seen the ghost himself, he told me, but his wife had definitely felt a black mood in the kitchen from time to time, and Little Jeb, a Parson's Terrier who elected not to move from the couch during my tour of the apartment, was highly sensitive to the spirits.

Did Little Jeb look traumatised by hauntings? It was difficult for me to judge, even though I consider myself as having a good understanding of canine body language. He certainly looked a little nervous, or sad maybe.

"One builder downed his tools," said Jeb, "walked off site, and never came back."[10]

---

[10] *I often walk by the apartments at The Ossington now and notice on these short winter days that the upper floors remain forever in darkness as if no-one lives there, and Rita has not yet come to The Writers Group as she promised she would. It leads me wonder, did I imagine visiting The Ossington during some autumnal delusion? Have I invented the famous painting truck driver? What if Jeb doesn't really exist? Or Little Jeb for that matter, sitting there, unwilling to dismount the furniture for fear of the Devil knows what? Are they all ghosts? I wonder, sometimes, do I have another story here? Usually, I make a small shuddering motion when I think of it and then banish such nonsense from my mind. Stick to writing about what actually happened at The Ossington, I scornfully remind myself.*

Greek Coffee
An Introduction at The Newark Book Festival

"You know there is a ghost in the cellars there, don't you?"

I first met Rita Hopkirk, the famous Saharan truck driver, at the Newark Book Festival one blazingly hot July afternoon last year.

"I live in the old ballroom at the Ossington," she had told me after introductions.

I was working The Writers Group stall in the Market Square at the time, playing my part in the rotation of members who were there to promote the group, sell our books, contribute to the success of the Book Festival, and do better than the rival writers groups from East Leake and Leicester by selling more books and signing up more members than they did. For my shift at the stall I had been paired with Sam, and as we were both new writers to the group we were a little bit nervous about being put in charge of the stall and the float. It seemed like an awful lot of responsibility for beginners, even if one of the Chief Writers had promised to look in on us frequently (probably to make sure we hadn't somehow accidentally set light to the canopy or grossly offended the Lord Mayor or Duke and Duchess of Newcastle or other dignitaries on their rounds), and the second Chief Writer had given us a demonstration on how to manage the float and how to attract new members to the group with cunning sales patter.

"I usually begin with the line, 'Are you a writer yourself?'" explained Chief Writer Nick, adding further techniques and lines depending on the forks in the conversation, like when a potential customer simply backs away muttering 'just looking' and you have to be extra sharp to reel them in. I first met Chief Writer Nick at the previous year's Book Festival, and I saw this time around, from the other side of the stall, precisely how I'd ended up in The Writers Group myself.

"Are you a writer yourself?" asked my colleague Sam, to the first person who came along that morning. She was a natural. What followed was a lengthy conversation with some hearty laughter that concluded with the sale of two anthologies of work by The Writers Group and an agreeable addition to the float. We decided on the balance of play that she would be the talker and I would handle counting out the change, propping up books that fell down in the wind, and pointing vaguely at anthologies in reference to whatever Sam happened to be telling passers-by at the time. Occasionally I would say 'hello' but I knew in my heart that I was not delivering with her easy aplomb, so I let the arrangement stand and she did most of the voice work. I knew that inevitably Sam would need a break from all the talking at some point though, and I would have to step up. Sure enough, she had just gone to pick up some takeaway coffees from the Green Olive when a glamorously bohemian older woman came to the stall and I was forced to begin a conversation without Sam's more capable assistance.

"Are you interested in writing?" I said, bungling the first line. It was a book festival. Of course she was.

I recovered sufficiently to outline the goings on of The Writers Group and some of the books we had produced over the years. In order to encourage her to sign up I also mentioned that we were presently engaged in the writing of a new collection on the historic buildings of Newark.

"I live in an historic building here myself," she told me, going on to explain that she lived in the precise same building I was researching at the time - the Ossington Coffee Palace.

"What a coincidence!" I said, with my first enthusiasm of the day.

(Was it obvious, in hindsight, that Rita was a famous truck driver and an astounding painter? Perhaps I could be forgiven for not guessing about the heavy goods vehicle. But certainly, she was a person of creative character who took an immediate interest in The Writers Group stall, and it was easy for me to assume she had remarkable powers, probably in the direction of the written word which would be well suited to our fortnightly meetings and the readings at Anthony's café. There was certainly a part of me that was calculating my increased standing with the Chief Writers for bringing such a talent on board, but mostly I was excited to catch a break in my research on what happened at The Ossington, almost from the source, one degree removed. She was immediately generous in offering to help me.)

"I could tell you a thing or two about that place," Rita said, and I picked up my pad and pen to begin some solid note-taking on the subject.

"One builder downed his tools, walked off site, and never came back. Never even collected his wages."

Viva Java
Leisure Time at The LetsXcape Together Café

I took a break from my research to meet my friend Anthony for a cup of coffee and a game of dice at the LetsXcape Together Café in the Buttermarket. As proprietor, his shop hours are as playful as the theme of his establishment and one never knows quite when to catch him open: he is the platform nine-and-three-quarters of the Market Square, but he defies the town's early-closing afternoons for that rare and precious thing - a coffee after dark[11].

Naturally Anthony thrashed me at several quick games including a hand of Viva Java, but a punchy ristretto and a large helping of tap water washed the dizzying effects of the gin away, and before long I was restored and ready for dinner.

---

[11] Opening both onto the Market Square and into the atmospheric colonnades under the Town Hall, the café is a cornerstone of the vibrant

revival of the historic Buttermarket, a Victorian covered arcade instigated by the town's Urban Sanitary Authority in the 1880s when the former shutts and shambles of the butcher's market became unpalatable to the town's gentleman-councillors in the upper halls during long hot summers, and untenable under the growing understanding of environmental health. It really did stink, by all accounts.

Despite the impressive Arcadian renovations of the time, indicative of the optimism of Victorian market capitalists everywhere and the Newark trading families in particular, the Buttermarket has been thralled to cycles of decline and rejuvenation right through to the present moment and the latest refurbishment - of the mezzanine - in the 2020s. Removing two rows of empty boutique shops in favour of a more open space operated by the county library service toward adult education, it seems - for the time being at least - that the ambitions Viscountess Ossington held for the people of Newark are still alive and actively observed a few hundred metres up the road from her coffee tavern.

I wonder if Anthony's café also fulfils a role Lady Charlotte would have approved of and was in part a precursor to - after all, The Ossington boasted an 'American bowling alley', the first of its kind in the town, and surely the working men of Newark, too poor and too busy or too drunk to otherwise have time for board games, would have been catered for at the sober facility with games of Draughts, Chess, Merels, Hoppity, Taffle, Backgammon and of course Snakes & Ladders as diversionary and developmental activities - the Victorians, after all, loved their board games. (Dice and cards on the other hand, associated with vice and gambling, would certainly not have been available as magistrates listings of the time often featured convictions for both publicans and players leading to fines, closures, and possibly a session in the stocks for recidivist gamblers.) Anthony carries an enormous quantity of board games, card games, dice games, tabletop war games and even vintage video console games of which he is ever happy as custodian to introduce you to and thrash you at over a delightful Stokes of Lincoln-blended americano. The LetsXcape Together Café is Newark's first board game café in an age when such games might be seen in relief to the demon internet and all its unregulated and solitary vices.

Not particularly acquainted with this modern cultural phenomenon, I came to know the café and Anthony because the Writers

The Pizza Chef
An Italian Thin-Crust Sourdough Recipe

This is a section of the story in which I have failed to source adequate information and so must leave unwritten.

To explain: I wrote to The Zizzi Corporation with a friendly request for some commentary about their time as tenants in the Ossington Coffee Palace, but my email was ignored. Or feasibly my email remains low in a pile of emails

---

Group hold their monthly socials there on a certain regular evening - of which you can get full details if you subscribe to the group's newsletter or tap up the Chief Writers. Other groups taking advantage of the space for meetings and activities include the Still Life Drawing Group, the Radio Club, the War Gamers Group, the Future Technology War Gamers Group, the Fantasy War Gamers Group, The Life Drawing Class, The Painters Group (Watercolours and Pastels Division), The Historical Society Civil War Re-Enactment Committee and a Gala of Steam Punks. As a poet, I have been discussing founding a Poetry Group there with Anthony but so far have not been able to overcome my personal dislike of poetry or indeed most poets. Rhyming couplets and navel-gazing notwithstanding, the Viscountess would surely be delighted with the cultural engagement fostered by Anthony and his wonderful team of barista hosts at the LetsXcape Together Café, though what she would make of the Life Drawing Class (or the Steam Punks, for that matter) is anyone's guess.

It was through our meetings of The Writers Group that I also discovered more or less the only opportunity for a coffee in town after Early Closing Weekdays and Weekends. To give my frequent visits to 'the Escape' some semblance of legitimacy during this time of research, I often played Viva Java, a dice and card strategy game in which players attempt to become head of a commercial coffee empire. It is tremendous fun and Anthony is very good at it.

forwarded to the company historian, who is a long way from reading it because she has been inundated with requests for information and is struggling to keep on top of demand, especially since she might have only recently returned from a bout of sick leave on account of her condition - her legs perhaps, or her digestion, or her kidneys, or her inner ear and her balance, or her joints: all things which at times have bothered me and cause me to have the utmost sympathy for her, if that is the case. Maybe she'll get round to answering me one day, when it is too late and this essay about what happened at The Ossington is already published and probably lacking a critical detail which she may have furnished, if it weren't for her legs.

As I told my friend Galloway, I had hoped the corporation might've put me in touch with a Zizzi Chef, an eye-witness of sorts who could've told me all about the kitchen and the staff and the customers and the coffee-making appliances they utilised for the restaurant.

"By coincidence," said Galloway, "I do happen to know of a former junior chef who worked down there, had a lot of trouble with Wednesdays."

He was fired, Galloway told me, because he kept missing his midweek shifts on account of coming to believe that Wednesdays were not real. Galloway offered to put us in touch, as soon as he could recall his details. I didn't press him on the matter as it sounded familiar, like a story he had once told me in The Local Tap some miles out of town about an Icelandic fisherman who developed an intolerance of afternoons and began to fear his days were foreshortening. Sensing my reluctance, Galloway came up with a better solution.

"A recipe in the middle of a story sounds like an interesting digression," he said, adding "being only a junior chef he probably wouldn't have had much to say anyway."

I wrote to The Zizzi Corporation with a friendly request for a pizza recipe, but my email was ignored again so here is one of my own:

THE COSTELLO SAUCE SOURDOUGH

Add half a cup of water to half a cup of flour, make sure the water is unchlorinated, stir gently and leave with an air-breathing cap like a coffee filter for one day in a warm place. First thing next morning, add a tablespoon of flour and a tablespoon of water to the mix - this is called feeding. Feed by the same amount four or five times on the first day. Stir well each time. Next day, add about half a cup of each, flour and water, two or three times. Feed two tablespoons of each for the next seven days. When it shows bubbles it is active; remove or gently stir in any liquid gathering on the top. Place a clean cheesecloth over the jar and refrigerate, feed once a month by removing from fridge and placing a tablespoon of flour and one of water twice over the course of the day, and then refrigerate again. Continue to feed monthly for a minimum of two years, and then activate for baking:

Remove from refrigerator and feed, two or three times a day over the next 48 hours. The last feed should be bedtime before kneading day. On kneading day, mix one and a half cups of unbleached flour with a teaspoon of salt. Add one and a half cups of the sourdough (now properly called the sourdough starter) and four tablespoons of olive oil and form into a doughy ball. Knead until soft and drizzle with oil, leave to rest for eight hours, then refrigerate for three days. Make authentic Costello Sauce using sun-dried tomatoes, tomato purée, chopped basil and garlic, one red chilli, a little garlic butter (melted) a dob of black olive pesto and a generous smattering of Henderson's Yorkshire Relish. Grease a pie pan with olive oil and gently flatten out the dough into a thin layer. Apply the Costello Sauce, add thin slices of Welsh goat's cream cheese finished in rosary ash, and cook in a hot oven for 9 minutes. Serve with olives, still water and a double espresso, dark Italian roast.

Later as an afterthought I wrote to The Zizzi Corporation again, requesting information on their procurement policy and specifically where they got their coffee from. I thought it was the least they could do to help, although I didn't say as much for fear of offending or being ignored or filed as junk or labelled as a spammer or an idiot. But as it happened my email was ignored anyway. Or feasibly my email remains low in a pile of emails forwarded to the company coffee buyer, who is a long way from reading it because she always has more important emails to deal with first.

Flat White
A Conversation at The Prince Rupert

I took a break from my research to meet my friend Ade for dinner at The Prince Rupert, where we had a catch up on the progress of our different writing projects.

A favourite on the Civil War History Trail for its apparent connection to the prince who came to the relief of the town during a parliamentarian siege of 1644, the original Tudor building on Stodman Street has been expertly restored to preserve one of the oldest buildings in the town and make it a much appreciated venue for a substantial and high quality English roast dinner. We both went for the pork plate. For all the original wooden beams and sensitive plastering to open up two floors of hostelry, and a delicious apple sauce, what pleases me the most on my visits here is the array of nineteenth and twentieth century signage liberally hung on the lower floor walls to present a fabulous exploration of advertising design for butchers, brewers and cigarette makers and the rich adventure through typography that goes with it.

As always the pork was delicious, and well-fortified by a glass of Chilean Malbec.

I first met Ade at The Writers Group. We'd both joined at a similar time and for similar reasons - somewhere to go where we could talk about our unfinished novels and perhaps get them kick-started again. We found mutual interests in the literature of the American wild west, in air shows and air fields, war planes, The War, stories about The War, nostalgia for a boyhood as the children of people who had lived through The War, the trials and tribulations of our grown-up sons, the variable joys of mediocre football and the constant joy of Malbec, The Beiderbecke television trilogy, pub quizzes, radio drama, vintage comic books about The War, metal detectors, the villages of Elton, Shelton, Orston, Syerston, Car Colston and countryside surrounding, the experience of divorce, fragments of industrial machines, coffee, antiques and in particular small and useless artefacts, Putin's War, second-hand books, old maps and diagrams, living in Lewisham in the early Nineties, pub lunches, pub decor, pubs in general and writing. In the short time that I have known him The Writers Group seems to have assisted Ade in finding the spark for his novel, which he reports to be blossoming under the pen. (The Writers Group has assisted me too, in eventually accepting that I had actually abandoned my novel twenty years ago and just hadn't admitted it to myself yet. I have spent the intervening years talking about it with friends or acquaintances over coffee without getting a single word down on the page. Thanks to the generous support of The Writers Group, I have officially given up now.)

After a pleasant meal, I ordered a filter coffee. I'm not sure why.

Ade requested a flat white. The waitress frowned and tried out the sound of it. "A flat white," she ruminated, "flat white". She told us she'd have to check with the kitchen "if they have any of that", and ambled off. I thought she seemed rather irritated with Ade.

While she was gone finding out, Ade told me about The Committee of Adjustment, and his search for a suitable building that may have housed them - for his story of the same name. Thinking about what happened at The Ossington, I wondered if the Committee could've operated there when the government adjusted its purpose, since it had been requisitioned for a war effort which did not, apparently, include sitting about drinking coffee whilst listening to lectures by academics, autodidacts, polemicists, tautologists and the anti-vaccination movement.[12] I thought the whole concept of the Committee was a brilliant foundation for a story, and found myself suddenly quite anxious about my own research, and where it might take me, and just how interesting I could make the temperance movement for a general audience. I was experiencing a sort of writers envy for Ade's good idea but also a nagging insecurity[13]. Galloway loomed large in my imagination just then, and I thought about making the whole thing up, based on one of his many erroneous conceits.

---

[12] The records at the town library show a busy schedule of lectures for many years at the Coffee Palace, something which would no doubt have delighted Lady Charlotte, who died in 1889 only six years after the completion of her 'tavern', as she called it. Listings for the early lecture series include a diverse range of subjects across the sciences, arts, history, philosophy and politics such as would delight even a modern audience had the Coffee Palace remained in the possession of the town, including the relief of women from domestic coercion and violence, the almost limitless potential for hemp farming, and the dangers of vaccination. In this particular field, there seems to have been an ongoing rivalry for several years between two camps - The Anti Vaccination League held their first lecture there within a year of the Coffee Palace opening, and sound like the more hard-line of the rivals supporting a dogmatic and

The waitress came back with my coffee.

"We don't do them flat whites," she told Ade, brusquely, again giving off an air of having been offended by the request, "that's a MacDonald's thing apparently - you'll have to go there for one of them.

"I can do you some normal coffee with milk," she said.

Ade had some normal coffee with milk.

A Thing That Happened Near Here
A Reading at The LetsXcape Together Café

"He never ever came back, not even to collect his wages… and now the fates had caught up with The Lady, and here she was," read Rita from her handwritten paper, dramatically, "in the cellar under the kitchen, in the haunting company of her painted likeness, looking down austerely from the wall. It was a moment when all the shifting sands of her life (and death) were washed smooth by the ebb and flow of time. It was the crux, the culmination, the final whelm of the tide."

After dinner, Ade and I had dropped in on The Writers Group social meeting back at 'the Escape'. The dozen or so listeners around the table at the workshop applauded politely and nodded appreciatively at Rita's haunting recital. She

---

blanket disapproval of this most modern of medical applications, whilst the Society Against Compulsory Vaccination were apparently not wholly opposed to the needle, but just didn't like being pushed around.

[13] When I described detailed plans for this essay over refreshments at Stray's Café on Middle Gate with my partner, who is neuro-atypically direct, she sipped her mochaccino thoughtfully and said, "it sounds really… boring."

folded her paper and slipped it between the pages of a notebook.

"Well," said Nick, breaking a contemplative silence, "we liked that, didn't we?"

"For sure," agreed several members of the writer's workshop. "Real nice, Rita" said one.

"And look who's back!" said Nick, turning to Martin. "It's Martin! We haven't seen you for a while, Martin."

"Oh, you know," said Martin, "I've been busy, is all.

"We're all glad to have you back, fella!"

"Real nice," said someone.

"Since you've been busy and all," said Nick, "did you get time to write something down for us?"

"Well," said Martin, flicking through his notebook, "I've got this little thing here, it's not much, about - "

As Martin gave a précis of his story, the café owner Anthony brought an extra-shot americano (black, no sugar) to the table, which Martin had ordered when he arrived.

"Oh, that's interesting," said Nick, when Martin finished his summary, "like that thing, y'know… that happened near here, up at The Ossington wasn't it?"

"I know what you mean," said Martin, "yes I suppose that could've inspired me, I guess. Maybe."

"Well then," said Nick, "will you read it for us?"

"I suppose I could," said Martin. "It's not much, you know, not by Rita's standard - but if you're sure?"

"Come on now, Martin," said Nick, "don't be shy, this is an open table - we all like to hear your little stories, don't we, writers?"

"For sure," agreed several members of the writer's workshop. "Real nice," said one.

"Okay then," said Martin, "here it is, I suppose. It's called:

and bound by CPI Group (UK) Ltd, Croydon, CR0 4YY
21/06/2024
01013929-0004